Wolf and Owl Remember...

TRAVELS THROUGH TIME

ANTOINETTE SARCINELLA

COVER ART AND ILLUSTRATIONS
JOSEPH WOLVES KILL

PAGE PUBLISHING, INC.
Conneaut Lake, PA

First originally published by Page Publishing 2020

A portion of the proceeds of this book will be donated to support the Ness of Brodgar Trust in Orkney, Scotland.

ISBN 978-1-64701-615-9 (pbk)
ISBN 978-1-64701-616-6 (digital)

Printed in the United States of America

DEDICATION

My memory does not go back to a time without the wonder
of words. The world would have been smaller, with less color
and light, had I not heard amazing stories introducing me to
people and places beyond here, beyond now…beyond beyond:

To Oz, the Enchanted Forest, Shangri La,
Narnia, Middle Earth and Hogwarts.
To fairies, mermaids, dragons and the second star to the right.

This book is lovingly dedicated to the
guardians of those special places:
To the storytellers of every land who faithfully
preserve myth, legend and imagination.
To my children and grandchildren, to those who came before
and those yet to arrive who will carry on this ancient tradition:
Before you close your eyes each night… weave a little magic.

PART 1

Kumi

PROLOGUE

The world is changing quickly, and we have forgotten how important the earth at our feet should be. It can tell stories long forgotten. It was here during the time when the animals ruled this earth with wisdom greater than mankind can ever hope to have. It can remind us of the clear waters, the brilliance of a sunset free from smoke and pollution. The rocks are the oldest of the Creator's gifts; they remember what we have long forgotten.

Have you ever wondered how it would be if there was one, just one, who could be given the task of reminding all of us of our responsibility to the future generations of the world? Perhaps it would only be through returning to yesterday that we would come to understand and protect the future.

The circle could begin again....

CHAPTER 1

First Steps

Kumi stood silently as he watched the sea begin to change. The clouds rolled in, black and silver, taking command of the night sky. Slowly the drops began to fall. They turned into a steady stream, washing away the last remaining fractured light from the day.

He sat down on the hilltop as he watched the angry waves. Brilliantly lit in the flashes of lightning, the mountains of water fell to the gray sand below. He sighed as he realized it was time to take the first steps; it was time to go home.

Kumi had set out at daybreak with his empty day pack strapped across his back. He knew the path through the forest that lead to the water's edge; he had traveled it many times since he had first learned to walk. But today was the first time he had been old enough to go alone to gather the drift wood that washed up during the late summer storms.

He had been so excited he had scarcely slept the night before. It was still dark when he sat up from his sleep robes. He was ready. He knew there was work to do, and he knew he needed to get started.

"I will work hard, and I will be careful," he promised as he set out for the beach.

He had worked through the morning, stopping at midday to eat the lunch his mother had sent along. After eating he laid back on the sand, looking up into the endless sky, seeing gray-and-white clouds as they began to gather overhead.

"I wonder what clouds feel like? Can birds see through them? How do they know where they are going when clouds surround them? I wonder how it feels to step off the top of the highest tree, spread your wings, and float like a bird."

He wished he could lay there, dreaming of life as a bird, flying high above the seas, but he remembered his promise. He sighed as he stood up and went back to his chore.

Kumi walked slowly through the forest, carefully avoiding the dried leaves and small twigs that crumble beneath a child's eager footsteps. His parents had long ago taught him the value of silence as he traveled the well-worn paths leading home.

The day had been long and tiring. He was almost there. His feet began to move more quickly, his mind wandering to the warmth and safety of home, his mother waiting, dinner cooking. He looked straight ahead, not noticing the small form breathing soundlessly as he walked toward her.

The little bird laid, crumpled at the base of the giant oak tree, her wing bent at a painful angle. Half hidden by the dead leaves she sensed his approach. She watched carefully and then decided.

"Little boy," she said. "I need help." He was startled by the sound. He looked behind him. Nothing. He took another step. Again a small voice spoke softly, "Little boy."

He looked. Still nothing. He saw only trees as he gazed deeply into the forest in search of the voice.

"Down here."

Then that he saw her, concealed among the leaves and dying weeds. He bent down, slowly reaching out to uncover the tiny creature.

"Was that you talking?" he asked, forgetting, for a moment, the bird's injury.

"Yes, does that surprise you?"

"But birds can't talk."

"Of course we can. In a time, not so long ago, we all spoke and walked and lived as one on this earth."

"Then why haven't I ever spoken with a bird before?"

The bird seemed lost in thought. "Men stopped listening to us a long time ago. They wanted to rule the earth, but they had stopped loving it. We never stopped talking to you. You simply stopped listening to us."

Kumi gently lifted the injured creature, cradling the broken wing in his hands. He bent over and carefully examined the break.

"I think I can fix this," he murmured as he placed the tiny bird safely on top of his daypack. "But first, we need to get home."

"How did you fall from the tree?" Kumi was curious. "Were you trying to fly?" Before the little bird could answer, Kumi looked at her seriously. "Why is it you can fly? Why can't I?"

She smiled to herself, thinking, *Here is one who wants to learn. He is young and will have many winters to pass on the lost wisdom we animals still possess. Perhaps he is the one chosen to show the way to the others. He must be the one sent for us to teach.*

"There are many stories from long ago that tell how each of us came to be. The stories tell of our brotherhood and our brave battles to save this world for the generations to follow. Since you have cared for my broken wing, I would like to help heal your broken bonds with the spirits of all living creatures. We can travel to other times and places where you could learn many lessons. I will take you if you want to journey back with me."

Kumi looked solemn. It sounded so exciting. He would travel and learn about strange lands and places. But what about his family and friends? Would he ever see them again? Would he be different when he returned?

He had heard there were many things that had changed for his people as the hunting seasons had passed since the time of his grandfathers and their grandfathers before them. He had heard of others, people from faraway lands and tribes with different customs and ways. He nodded.

"I think it's a journey I would like to take. If you lead the way, I will follow."

CHAPTER 2

The Choice

Kumi greeted his mother as he entered the lodge. He placed the little bird in a warm spot, safely tucked into a blanket near the open fire. Their faces were bathed in the shadows, dancing to a silent drumbeat. He sat down, crossed his legs, and waited. The bird began to speak.

"The stories go back to a time long ago, or not so long ago, for you must remember this earth is very old. It has been here since before the light and will remain long after the light turns once again to darkness. But it is the light that brings life to those things waiting deep beneath the surface.

Those who shared the earth during the old time knew the truth. They respected their world and knew they must work together to protect it. For us to understand how we have come to live as we do, it is necessary to look at those early beginnings when the earth was new and filled with promise."

Kumi's face shone in the firelight as he listened to the gentle words of his new friend. Slowly the shadows began to fade around him. He found himself in a forest glen, surrounded on all sides by the creatures of the earth. He saw the bear and the buffalo, the eagle and the hawk. He looked at those who lived in the sky and those from beneath the sea. He knew he was ready to begin.

"For any long journey, we must make plans and have guides," the bird explained. "You may choose your guides to take you into their world and tell you how all things came to be connected. They will tell you how the balance was lost and help you reach into the future once you have come to understand the past."

Kumi sat in silence. He looked around the circle, unsure of his choice, yet knowing its importance. Then he saw them, side by side, sitting apart from the others, two creatures of the night forever connected in the darkness to one another. From different worlds, but watching together, were the wolf and the owl.

He remembered his grandfather's words not so very long ago. "At night there are voices, voices that call to one another. Though many animals come awake when the rest of us sleep, there are only two who will reach out, calling out to warn and guide the others. Listen in the darkness, Kumi, and you will hear the cry of the wolf and the owl calling out her answer. The others walk the night in silence. You will never know they are there. Wolf and Owl still call out, letting all who can hear them know they have command of the darkest night."

"I choose Wolf and Owl," he spoke with confidence. "They can see into the darkness when others need light. They will keep me from getting lost as I travel this unknown world."

Wolf and Owl stepped forward and stood in front of the small boy. "We are honored by your trust in us. You have decided you want to be the one to bring light to the future. We will now begin our journey to find the answers you will need."

CHAPTER 3

The Journey Begins

Far to the east a small ember seemed to glow in that single thread where the sky bends to meet the morning earth.

Kumi placed his hand lightly on Wolf's head, stroking the soft gray fur. Owl flew high into the treetop and looked into the dark night. Effortlessly floating on the gentle breeze, she returned to earth, settling on Kumi's shoulder.

"We go east," she said, "to where a great ocean greets each new day."

The winds began to rise, ruffling the feathers on Owl's shoulders. The travelers were lifted high into the night sky, silhouetted against the silver moon. The forest began to fade as they rose higher and higher, and soon the clouds were all around them. Lost within the snowy white, his guides began to speak.

"I am Wolf," said a deep voice from beneath his hand. "I walk by night and sleep by day. I hunt for the pack and provide for all those in my care. Man has forgotten his responsibility to provide for those weaker or younger than himself. He thinks only of his own needs. Wolves live to provide for the pack, and that is my destiny as well. My oldest friend now sits on your shoulder. Though she is of the sky and I am of the earth, nothing can destroy our friendship. As we are connected, so are the earth and sky of this world. As we are different, so are they, yet one cannot exist without the balance of the other."

"I am Owl." The voice was soft in Kumi's ear. "I fly in the night sky, seldom seeing the light of day. I am thankful for this time I will share you with you and Wolf. Together we can take you to the hearts of the people of yesterday. There you will learn the wisdom we shared long ago. Your choice of us as your guides is a good one. It gives us the chance to show you the connection each of us has to the future of our world."

Slowly the clouds began to part, and the winds calmed around them. As they were gently set down, Kumi saw before him an unending ocean, dark and frightening under the pale moon. He held tightly to Wolf, fear taking over his young mind.

"Look," Owl spoke to Kumi, hoping to calm his fears.

Behind him he saw the firelight, beckoning him from the darkness. The travelers walked toward the flames and the welcoming sounds of voices speaking by the fireside.

The fire warmed them as they approached, and Kumi felt himself relaxing. Voices called out, urging them to join the gathering. As Kumi looked through the darkness, he saw faces that looked much like those he had known throughout his short life, and he was comforted.

"They look just like me, like my family and friends. I thought they would be different. We have come such a long way."

Owl smiled at the child; the lessons needed to begin.

"People are the same and different no matter where or when you travel. The people of long ago were much like you, and they were also very different. Those you will meet on our journey will teach you many things if you are willing to learn. The most important of your lessons will be those you learn from people whose ways may seem strange to you."

As Owl finished speaking, she turned to Wolf. "Take Kumi to sit with the people of the east, they are waiting for him by the fire. He must meet these people of the eastern lands, or he will never truly begin the journey to understanding. Each of them has many stories, but our time here is short. I will choose his teacher here among the wise ones who remember what others have forgotten."

CHAPTER 4

The Grandmother's Lesson

Kumi looked around the circle, at the faces glowing bronze from the flames. Wolf watched quietly, standing guard in this unfamiliar place. Suddenly Owl appeared, sitting on the arm of the eldest of the grandmothers.

She spoke to the boy, "My people come from the warm southern lands of the east, where our relatives have long made their homes. Some of the answers lie here, in the wisdom of long ago. You need only to ask, and the door will open."

"Grandmother," the boy said softly, "I have come to learn." He sat down by her side, waiting for his journey to begin.

"Little one, the first lesson you must learn on this journey is all creatures must care for themselves in this life. Once we learn to take care of ourselves, we will then gain the strength to care for all living creatures. Hard work and careful thought are two of the gifts we can give back to the Creator who has given us so much.

In the early times, when the earth was new, a careless locust traveled our lands. He stopped not far from here and watched an ant hard at work. "Come dance with me," the locust said, but the ant continued his chores.

"'Can't you see I am busy? I have to gather my food and build my house for the winter. I will have time to dance and play when I have prepared for the cold months ahead.'"

The ant worked throughout that day and the days that followed. Soon he had leaves and plants stored for the winter and a cozy home for when the winds began.

The locust laughed as he watched. "I will worry later. Today all I want to do is dance."

He kept dancing and laughing as the days turned from one into another.

One morning, as the sun awoke in the east, the locust saw that there was a light coating of frost on the ground. He tried to dance but slipped on the icy earth.

The locust walked by the ant's warm home and looked inside. The ant was resting safely, surrounded by all the food he had collected during the last days of summer. But the sun began to shine, the frost melted away, and the locust smiled happily as he continued to dance away the last days of autumn.

As the days grew colder and the food grew scarce, the ant could be seen dancing and laughing in his warm little house. Finally, the locust came to his door, begging to come in out of the cold and have something to eat.

"I told you, didn't I? There is a time to dance, and there is a time to work and plan for your needs. If you don't plan to care for yourself, you will never be able to help those who are weaker or younger."

Kumi listened, nodding as he began to understand the message hidden in the story.

"Grandmother, I have seen many people who are like the locust. They are never busy. I have seen them as they lay by the stream or nap under trees. They do not chop wood. They do not hunt or fish. They are content to let the others in the village work for them. They always want someone else to provide for them. But there are also many like the ant. They take care of everyone, the children, the women, and the elders. Without their hard work, we would all be cold and hungry when the winter winds come. They seem happy. They sing in their lodges when the snow is falling, they laugh as they tell us stories during the long dark days, and they smile as they offer whatever they have to those of us they have sworn to protect.

Does their happiness come from what they have done for themselves, or from what they are able to do for the rest of us?"

The tiny woman patted Kumi's hand as it sat unmoving in his lap. "What do you think, child?"

"I think it must come from knowing they have worked hard and done what needed to be done. It's good to be able to take care of yourself. And it must be a special gift to be able to share with others."

Wolf looked at the faces of the people who listened from around the fire. He saw how they smiled at Kumi, and his spirit was lifted. He knew the child was going to learn many things. The journey had begun well. Soon it would be time to go on, but for now he was content to listen to the soft voices murmuring on into the dark night.

CHAPTER 5

Traveling On

Owl flew down from her lookout in the highest of the trees surrounding the village. She looked at the sleeping child and saw he was no longer the small boy she had brought to the fireside. He had grown during their time here and was now a young man.

"Wolf," she said as she landed on his strong back, "do you see how the child has grown? His search for knowledge has brought him a long distance, but now it is time to go forward again."

She knew they must leave the peace of the quiet village; there were still many answers waiting.

Wolf nodded. "In what direction does our journey take us now? Only you can lead us across the dark mountains and prairies. I can protect our traveler on this earth, but you rule the night skies."

"Wake up, little brother." The beating of her wings spoke like the pounding of the drums. "We go south, where the warm winds and the morning sun bring new life from the earth."

"But I feel safe here. I want to stay and learn more from the grandmothers. I am afraid to journey into the night again. There is danger in what we don't know."

"That is why we must go. Danger does not lie in what you do not know. It hides in what you will not learn. And there is much to learn." Wolf was ready for the journey, impatient to continue on their quest.

As Wolf spoke, the darkness wrapped around them, and Kumi was lifted once again into the night sky. No clouds appeared this time, and he watched the land as it fell away. He saw the village disappear, the village that had shared so much with a small child from another time.

CHAPTER 6

Friends through Time

Wolf spoke, "It is time for us to tell you the story of Wolf and Owl. It is filled with friendship and hope. There is sorrow as well, but that is the story of all living things. No life is complete without tears. Tears come with sadness, but they also wash that sorrow away until only the joy remains."

Owl flew down to his side. "Wolf has been with me through many lifetimes. We have traveled together before. But in this lifetime, we have different paths, his leads across the land while I live on the wind."

Wolf continued the story, "In a time long gone by, Wolf and Owl were companions, traveling by night when the world slept. How these bonds were formed is our story."

Kumi sat quietly as Wolf spoke. He wanted to hear the story of his two friends. He needed to understand how they came to be together, guiding each step on his long night's journey.

"In a forest not far from here, Wolf and his pack lived, keeping to themselves, looking for food and shelter.

One day Wolf went out to hunt. He remembered the day he was given the responsibility of leading the pack. He paused briefly, thinking back to his first hunt when he was young. He had gone with the others of his family, watching and learning. He knew there was danger, but he knew that now many lives depended upon his success.

Suddenly he felt eyes watching him. There was a new and unknown danger ahead. He turned quickly, but it was too late. There was a sound like a loud crack of thunder and a puff of smoke. Wolf felt a hot pain in his leg, and he fell silently to the ground below.

He tried to move, but the pain was too great. He waited, listening, but the forest was quiet and still.

Wolf felt very tired. He slept. He did not feel the cold wind. He did not know a great snow was coming. Wolf laid there many hours, lost in a dreamless sleep.

He awoke suddenly, feeling the cold dampness through his heavy coat. He knew he had to find shelter from the bitter wind and blinding snow.

A short distance away he saw a spot that would work. At the base of a giant tree, a root lifted out of the ground. Using his front paws, he began to pull himself toward the tree. He moved a little then tried again.

Slowly he dragged himself to the great tree. With his last remaining strength, he pulled himself to safety. As he fell back into the world of dreams, Wolf prayed the Great Spirit would protect his pack until he returned.

The Great Spirit heard his prayer and looked down on the injured Wolf.

Pulling a small feather from his hair tie, he let it fall. It landed in the snow-covered tree above Wolf. The feather suddenly began to change, turning into a great White Owl shaking out her wings. She hooted softly as she looked down, understanding exactly what she needed to do. She had to protect Wolf from the cold winds and the spreading blanket of snow. She lifted off the branch, drifting silently down to the fallen Wolf. She covered him with her wings to protect him against the cold.

As morning approached, Owl left Wolf alone to hunt for food. Bringing back a small rabbit, she carefully fed the half-waking Wolf.

Wolf did not have the strength to open his eyes, but he knew he was not alone. Owl continued to care for him for several days. At night she protected him from the cold, hunting for food when Wolf rested quietly in his deepest sleep.

One morning Wolf awoke. He was stiff and still felt some pain, but he knew he would soon be himself again. He knew he had not been able to hunt, yet he was not hungry. And why was he warm and dry? He tried to remember.

Wolf tried to move and succeeded in standing on shaky legs. There was a voice from above. "Do not move too quickly. You have been ill for many days."

Wolf looked up into the tree rising high above him. He didn't recognize the gentle voice. He searched through the half-light of the tree until he met a pair of eyes in the shadows. Someone was there.

"I am glad to see you can stand once again, my friend."

As the next days and nights passed, Wolf began to understand what had happened. Wolf now knew the snow he thought had covered him as he laid beneath the tree was the powerful white wings of his friend.

Wolf and Owl watched over one another as they traveled through the forest. Time passed swiftly. One day Owl told her companion she must return to he who had sent her. 'Wolf, do not ask how I know the time has come, only know it has. I must go home. Never forget our friendship. Always remember how two creatures from different worlds lived together for this time in peace.' With that, she spread her white wings and flew silently into the setting sun.

Wolf stood, watching but not wanting to believe she was gone. He called after her, asking her to stay. But she was gone, and all he could think of was finding her once again.

Wolf searched the land for Owl. He traveled many miles through the blackest nights, always looking for his dearest friend.

Today Wolf still searches for his lost companion. You can hear him calling in the forest if you listen. There are times he thinks he sees her high in the night sky. He goes to a clearing and, looking up, he sees the silver moon. It is big and round as though one of her eyes is staring at him in the starlit sky. He listens for her in the dark night, hoping to hear her answer."

Kumi looked deep into Owl's eyes, round as the moon glowing in her midnight sky. He saw only his own reflection, but then, slowly, faintly, something else appeared. He could see her gentle, loving spirit.

Kumi now understood the bond between his guides. They lived in separate worlds, but those worlds were forever connected. He knew that somewhere in their story was the answer to an important question. How could man and beast live together and share the earth? If these two creatures from different worlds could find each other, then he was sure he could find his answer too.

"Help me to understand." Kumi was not certain how to ask this of his new friends. "Why does is have to be like this? Why can't you be together?"

"We cannot ever hope to understand all that the Creator has done here. There are reasons why all things occur on this earth. Some things teach us, others will lead us to answers at another time. We will not know all the answers until our journey is complete. Then we will be united, understanding those things we have learned together. Then we will walk our paths as one again."

As Owl spoke, she sat on Wolf's shoulder. He slowed his pace so she would not fall from her perch. The wind silenced around them, and the earth reached up to greet them.

CHAPTER 7

Bringing the Sun

The green of the rolling southern hills was soft beneath their feet, cushioning them as they fell to earth. The warmth of the summer night was welcoming, and Kumi was now anxious to continue the journey.

A trail wound through the brush, tracing the hilltops to a village in the distance. They walked in silence, each deep in thought.

The village was alive with excitement—Wolf and Owl had returned. It had been many winters since the night travelers had visited. They brought a young man this time, a stranger. Few strangers ever walked these trails; few unknown faces had been seen by the people of the southern lands.

"We have brought Kumi. He comes from a time when the people have lost their way. He has come to learn what you of this time understand. He is searching for lost knowledge."

When he finished speaking, Wolf sat to the side of the elders. His eyes looked for Owl, and he nodded slightly.

She flew on silent wind to the rocks beside the riverbank. She stretched her wings then wrapped them around herself.

"Kumi has grown in wisdom but must continue to search. We ask your elders to share the wisdom of their winters so he may learn the truth and return with it to his own time."

Her eyes rested upon the tiny grandmother seated next to Kumi. She smiled slightly, understanding the request.

Reaching out her hand, she took Kumi's and said, "Here your journey continues. It is time to see the yesterdays of all people, to learn from their ways and their vision.

In that time, long before men came to this earth, the world was a dark and frightening place. The animals knew, in order for there to be a good life, there must be light and dark, but there was only darkness. Deep within the earth there was a great light and warmth. The animals called this light 'the sun.' They wanted to bring that great light up so all the earth could share in the warmth.

All the animals gathered together in a great council. They knew they must take a piece of the sun for themselves. Then they would place it in the sky where all could share in its beauty.

"I will go and steal a piece of the sun," Fox told the gathering. He ran off into the dark cave that led to the place where the sun slept. Breaking off a piece of the sun, he began to run from the cave, carrying it in his mouth. But the sun's bright glow grew hotter and hotter, and before long, Fox had to drop the smoking cinders that burned his mouth. That is why, even today, the fox has a black mouth.

"'Let me go,' offered Possum. He ran deep into the cave and, finding the sun where Fox had told him, he carefully picked up a cinder in his bushy tail. He began to run. As he ran, he did not notice the sun had burned through his thick fur and fallen out. To this day, Possum has a naked tail because long ago the sun had burned the fur to nothing.

Buzzard had watched quietly, and now he spoke, "Even if you get the sun from the cave, it must go high into the sky if all are to share its gifts. I will go into the cave to bring the sun to the world. Then I will do what is needed to place it high in the sky for everyone's use." Buzzard flew deep into the cave and found the sun. He placed the burning ember on his head and began to fly. The embers burned the shiny black feathers on Buzzard's head. but he continued to fly. He emerged from the darkness and soared high into the sky. The ember burned hotter now, but Buzzard knew what must be done. The feathers on his head were gone, and his skin had seared to a dark red, but Buzzard flew higher and higher. At last he reached the top of the sky, and he carefully placed the sun at the highest peak.

Buzzard would never again have feathers on the top of his head, the skin remaining the deep red of the sunset.

But Buzzard was honored by the Creator for his courage and his hard work. He would always fly higher than the other birds, soaring closest to the sun he had placed so carefully in the shimmering sky above the earth."

Grandmother smiled down at Kumi. "Tell me, what have you learned from your brothers in this story?"

Kumi thought for many moments. In his mind, he watched Fox and Possum as they struggled to succeed for the good of all the animals. He could see Buzzard flying high into the dark sky, carrying the first light of day. Slowly he began to understand the message hidden within the story.

"Grandmother, the animals fought to make the world a better place. They worked together at their own risk to help one another. Buzzard shared the great wealth of the sunlight with everyone, and the rewards are still ours today."

A smile lit her lined face. Her soft voice assured him he had understood. The animals knew they would survive and be strong by working together. They risked great danger, but their world was worth the challenge.

Kumi was lost in the grandmother's words, traveling swiftly through the days when all things were related. He closed his eyes, seeing Buzzard, Possum, and Fox as they tried to teach the people those things they knew so well.

"Grandmother, why can't people hear the lessons? Why do they look away when they should see the truth?"

She smiled at the young man. He was wise beyond his years. He had asked the questions; he needed the answers. Before her she watched as Kumi again grew older than when he had arrived. She saw a man, full grown and wise. She knew with certainty as he continued to search, he would continue to grow. It was good.

From the nearby shadows, the guides appeared to Kumi. Wolf approached slowly as Owl once again flew to the tops of the nearby trees. Shining white in the jet-black sky, she flew on the warm night air. She settled in the highest branch and began to turn her head slowly from side to side.

Her return was swift, her message clear. They would travel far to the west, where the sun sleeps as it awaits the dawning of each new day.

CHAPTER 8

Where the Sun Rests

The night had seemed endless. The travelers were beginning to weary. But there was still so much to learn; they pressed onward toward the sunset's horizon. As the sky lifted them once again, they moved forward, leaving the southern hills and gentle breezes behind them.

Kumi's hand rested on Wolf's back, feeling the tense muscles that had carried him on the winds of time. Owl flew ahead, never forgetting her duty to lead Kumi and Wolf safely through the darkness.

Soon the three began to walk, traveling slowly across the sands. Each step brought them closer to one another while taking them farther from all they left behind not so very long ago. They were careful as they continued their adventure. unsure of what lay ahead yet knowing the importance of the journey. Each searched for the unknown, seeking hope for the future. Yes, the journey was a good one, an important one.

"The western door reaches from the warmth of the southern lands to the coldest northern shores. The people of the west have had the gift of the endless ocean and its bounty since time began. They are the ones who guard the resting place of the sun each evening as it sinks below the dark horizon," Owl explained as they listened to the waves breaking along the ocean shoreline.

As they walked through the darkness, Kumi could see the stars reflected in the blackness of the ocean stretching before them. Far out he could see the shadows of the tiny islands across the water. Owl began to speak of the ones who had lived here since the beginning of time.

"The west has many people whose lives will seem strange to you. They live by the water, as your people have for many years. But even the waters of this earth are different, and you must learn to understand and honor that difference. These people have lived in harmony with the waters of the west for many generations. To the north they share the waters with the giant whales and the seals who live on the blue ice floating in the frozen sea. They are known by many names. They are the Tlingit, the Aleut, and the Kwakiutl. They are people of the west, but they are also people of the north. Many of them sleep in houses carved in ice and wear the warm fur of animals to keep from freezing in the winters that seem to have no end.

If we were to travel south from the frozen northern edges of the western gate, we would encounter others. There you would meet the Maidu, the Miwok, the Pomo, and the Wiyot. They, too, have their stories to share. They have a long history that tells us of time gone by when the world was new, and there was promise for all creatures willing to fight and work together. Long ago a grandmother of the west told me an ancient story. I was to remember it and share it with another when the time was right. Since you have chosen us to share this night's journey, I will repay that honor by sharing her story with you.

Kumi, all creatures walking this earth are the same. We are all different as well. The important thing to remember when you return to your time is, different as we are, we must all work together to protect our world. If we work together, we can conquer the greatest threats. If we fight amongst ourselves, we will lose the most important battles we face.

We have many things we take for granted in this world. There are things we see each day, but we never stop to think of the battles fought so we might have these gifts. You drink fresh water or eat fresh meat and fish. You lie beneath the spreading boughs of the giant oak when the sun is high on a summer day. The world was not always this way. Creatures of all walks of life fought together to give you these things. It was those things that make them the same that brought them together. But it was often their differences that helped them to triumph.

There was a time when the world was a dark and frightening place. It was always cold, and the people lived in caves, hiding from the wind and the darkness. They were afraid, for the nights were long, and the people felt as though life ended when the sun slipped below the horizon. Each night they would pray that the sun would wake again to save them from the long night.

Then the people found fire. Fire changed their lives, bringing warmth and light in the darkness. They had waited through generations and now were ready to use the fire wisely and well. They would gather around the fire while the sun rested. They would cook their food and sit as a family, sharing stories and comforting one another through the night.

But Thunder became angry. He wanted to be the only one to have fire. He remembered how it felt when he would shake the darkness as his brother, Lightening, would light up the sky for seconds before hiding once again. He wanted the power over the people so he could continue to rule the darkness with fear. If he could steal fire, it would be easy to rid the world of the people who had become the favorites of the Creator. His pride and jealousy would not allow him to share. He had to get the fire from the people.

He planned and schemed, and then one day he succeeded and took the fire, hiding it in his home far to the south. He thought the people were sure to die now. He thought of the children and the elders, sitting once again in the cold and dark. His jealous mind was happy.

But Thunder had not understood the strength of the people when they gathered together. They had learned much during their time in the warmth. Even though they could no longer cook their food or warm their homes, they continued to live. The people decided they should all live together in a big sweat lodge during this time so they could try to stay warm. They helped each other and shared what they had. They continued to survive, but they missed the warmth fire had brought to their lives.

One morning Lizard and his brother went outside early and sat, looking at the mountains all around. As they looked to the west, they were sure they saw smoke rising into the sky.

"'Come quickly,' they called to the others. 'We see smoke. Someone has fire!'

The others came running out when they heard the lizards yelling for them, but they didn't believe their story of the rising smoke. But the two insisted, pointing to the tiny white column of white rising far off in the distance. The others stared toward the horizon, and then they, too, realized there was smoke rising toward the sky.

'We must get the fire back,' one of the elders said, looking at everyone gathered outside the sweathouse. 'Who among you will challenge Thunder for the fire that will help us to live?'

Deer, Mouse, Skunk, and Dog each stepped forward. Each knew he had a different ability, and each was willing to face Thunder to help get fire back for the people. Mouse was tiny and could hide unnoticed, Deer was swift, Skunk was courageous and Dog was quick witted and intelligent. Together they traveled to Thunder's home high in the mountains of the west.

They watched from a distance and saw a tiny bird guarding the entrance to Thunder's home. Inside his daughters slept beside the fire he had stolen from the people. Mouse reached into the pack on his back and pulled out his flute. 'Stay here until I return,' he told his companions, and he scampered away.

When Mouse arrived at the door, he saw the watchful little bird had finally fallen into a deep sleep. He slipped past quietly and entered the home of the frightening Thunder. The daughters slept soundly by the warm fire burning inside.

Mouse carefully filled his flute with fire. He crept out of the house, rejoining the others waiting for his return. He split the fire in two, giving part to Dog and handing the rest, still tucked into his flute, to Deer. They both began to run toward home.

They were only partway home when Thunder returned home. He saw that some of his fire was gone, and he began to bellow in anger. Hearing their father, the sleeping daughters awoke and jumped up to run after him.

Thunder was chasing Deer and Dog, determined to get his fire back. They were almost home when they saw Skunk in the road ahead. He stepped aside as they raced past but then returned to his post in the middle of the path.

As Thunder approached, Skunk aimed his arrow, and with one perfect shot, Thunder fell to the ground. His daughters, following at some distance, saw their father drop as the arrow struck its mark. They stopped suddenly, looking at the brave Skunk standing in the path ahead.

"'Never come to this land again! You are sky beings, and that is where you must stay forever. Do not ever return and try to harm the people again!'

Hearing that, the daughters fled to the highest point of the sky. They have never again tried to harm the people, and the people have had fire from that time until today."

Kumi listened intently until Owl had finished her story. He walked quietly as he tried to understand the message hidden within the tale of how fire had come to the People.

"I have tried to work with my brothers, doing our chores together or working on a task our mother has given us. We always end up arguing. My oldest brother says he knows the right way, my other brother refuses to listen, and I am never sure who is right and who is wrong. Perhaps if we could learn the lesson of Dog, Mouse, Skunk, and Deer, we would finish our tasks in better humor than we have in the past. They all worked together, each using his greatest strength, and they were able to triumph over a powerful enemy."

CHAPTER 9

We Are All Related

Owl looked at Wolf and smiled. Wolf nodded, knowing Kumi had heard and learned. Power did not come from one fighting alone but from all who worked together, understanding all living creatures are related, and this family tie of the living must be honored.

"Kumi, we have brought you to our next resting place. The western door is found here as well, in the gentle south, where the people build homes from grasses and reeds they have gathered by the creek beds. Here the Chumash people have made their homes since the time they traveled here from across the water. They are the keepers of the western gate here in the south.

The people of this land are different than you, Kumi. But they are different than one another as well. Remember, as you learn from these people, they have known, for countless generations, differences are to be celebrated not to be feared."

The sand was warm beneath their feet as they approached the smiling people pulling nets from the water. As Kumi looked around, he saw these people were very different than those he had met before. They wore skirts made of grasses dried in the sun and necklaces of brightly colored shells. He looked at them in wonder, then turned to his guides.

"These people seem like my people, and yet they are not like us. How is it possible we can be so similar but different at the same time?"

Owl nodded as she listened to Kumi speak. She could see how much he was learning. His questions were good ones, and she knew he was waiting for answers. She flew to the side of the smiling woman sitting near the water's edge. Owl whispered in her ear, and she stood up slowly and walked toward the young man.

The woman took Kumi's hand and walked with him to the water's edge. Raising her other hand, she gestured to the blue water and the distant islands.

"What do you see when you look into the waters of the ocean or a mountain lake? Do you see that there lies beneath a life not so very different than your own? And when you look to the skies? Do you see the birds soaring and gliding on the silent wind? Do you greet them as your brothers? All of life is a great circle, my child, and it welcomes you as a relative."

Kumi listened as the grandmother spoke. He was lost in thought for a long time, his brow furrowed as he tried to find the words for the question forming in his mind.

"I have been taught all things in the world are related, but man has forgotten his connection to the others who share this world. But how can it be that we are related when the creatures of the earth are so different? Although they have been kind to me, and we have shared much together as we have journeyed, I cannot see my relation to Wolf and Owl. They have become my friends and my companions, but we cannot be related."

CHAPTER 10

The Dolphin People

The grandmother's eyes misted over as she thought back to the time so long ago when her people had become one with the creatures of the great oceans of the earth.

"I will share our secrets with you tonight because you have come a long distance, and your traveling companions have asked my help. We have trusted them for many years, and they have chosen you to learn those lessons that have been lost.

Long ago, when the world was very young, our people did not understand that all who walk this earth are connected. It was not until they were able to see with their own eyes that they came to understand man should not believe he rules the others on this earth. We must look at those who walk different paths with respect and hope they, too, will see us in a good way.

My people did not always live as they now do. We lived on the beautiful islands that dot the coastline in the western waters. One of these was the island called Limuw. This island had been the creation of the earth goddess, Hutash. Soon the island was covered with plants and living things, growing lush and beautiful in the bright, sunny days. Hutash then gathered the seeds of her most beautiful tree and scattered them across the island. When they opened, they were no longer plants, but living beings in her own image who were to be the beginning of the Chumash people.

One night she called Sky Snake to come and see the beautiful people she had placed on her island. Sky Snake looked down on the

Chumash people, and he loved them as Hutash did. He sent them a wondrous gift that evening. Wrapping himself in a robe of light, he opened his mouth and sent down a great bolt of lightning. The bolt struck and fire began to burn. Now the people had food to eat, fire to keep them warm, and a beautiful island to call their own. The people grew content on their island, fishing from their small boats and farming the land. One day there was a great storm that continued throughout the night and into the following days. When, at last, the rain and wind ended, the fish had left our waters. The people waited, but the fish never returned. Our people became weak from hunger, and soon they knew they would begin to die.

With nothing left to do, the people lit their fires, and as the smoke began to curl upward, they prayed to Hutash. The smoke carried their prayers higher than the eagle flies, and Hutash looked down on her people in sadness.

The earth goddess took pity on the people and sent a message saying they were to follow her directions and they would be safe. She was going to build them a wonderful bridge that would take them to the mainland, where there was game to hunt and land to farm. The fish were plentiful on the shores, and the people would once again grow strong.

That night the people went to sleep in peace, knowing when they woke, they would travel to safety. When the morning light began to brighten the sky, the people ran to the water's edge. There before them was an amazing sight, a rainbow bridge reached from their small island to the mainland far ahead.

As the people prepared for the journey far above the water, Hutash spoke to them. They were to cross quickly, but they were not to run. They must take care not to slip off the arc as they crossed the water. They were also told they must never look down to the water during the crossing. If they slipped off or looked down, they would fall to the water and drown.

The people understood, and the crossing began. The children laughed and played as they walked, and their parents tried to hurry them along. The crossing was long, and they wanted to reach dry land before night fell.

But children will always be children, as that is their role in this world. They played and ran as they crossed. Some of them began to slip along the rainbow bridge, finally falling from the edge toward the blue waters far below. As the parents watched their children begin to fall, they looked over the edge, and they too began tumbling toward the darkness below.

As they drifted through the sky toward the deep ocean, Hutash looked down on her people. Again, she was saddened and took pity on them. As they hit the waters of the western ocean, they were suddenly transformed. Each one, in turn, entered the water and became a beautiful dolphin. As the dolphins began to swim through the waters, their brothers on the rainbow bridge took great care that no others fell.

When the last of the people reached the mainland, they looked out to the ocean and saw the dolphins at play. They gave thanks to the earth goddess for saving the children and their parents in such an amazing way. Our people have always known that we have relatives who do not walk the earth as we do. They swim through the oceans, yet they breathe the same air that we breathe. They have a language that we cannot speak. There are many languages on this earth we do not understand, yet they are languages nonetheless.

If our people have these relations, can we fail to see that others may be related in similar ways? Perhaps the people of the east have relatives who fly through the skies as Owl does. We cannot know how we are all related, only that we are.

Respect all of life, Kumi. Remember the rainbow bridge and look on all living things as your relations for that is how our world will survive."

It was time again for the travelers to continue the journey. Kumi knew that Wolf and Owl had chosen well again. They had taken him to one who could help open his heart and mind to endless possibilities.

CHAPTER 11

The Northern Night

"We have one last stop before we return to your world, Kumi. We must go north, where life sleeps peacefully until the promised springtime. There we will find the bear, the fox, and bobcat as they search for shelter from the bitter winds of winter. Here we shall also find the people who live in harmony with these creatures. In this cold land, you might find the Cree and the Assiniboine, the Lakota and the Cheyenne. The Northern Plains are home to these people and to the others who walk this land."

Owl's voice was a whisper, words spoken only to Kumi's heart, for she saw he had grown tired from the long night.

Kumi snuggled deep into Wolf's thick coat, sharing his warmth, as the night grew dark and frightening. No clouds appeared before them; only a carpet of stars covered the skies. Wolf seemed to disappear, his dark fur blending into the blackness of the surrounding night.

Owl's silver wings reached wide as she soared high above the earth, leading her companions through the darkness. There was only silence as she reached back into a time long gone by. Kumi had grown, learning so much as they traveled. Wolf had carried the child, standing guard as he learned and grew. Now he bore the weight of the grown Kumi, the man of promise he had become.

Kumi would serve the people well. The faith of his guides would be fulfilled. Wolf and Owl looked to one another, knowing their journey was near its end.

"Soon, Wolf, we will part again," Owl was sad as she spoke the words she knew must be said. "This journey of ours is near its end. We have done well together, and we have helped the little one to learn and grow. He has become a fine man, and he will pass on the wisdom he has learned this night. He is a part of each of us, our mission on this earth, and our love for all living things. I, too, have learned lessons on this journey. I know I cannot live bound to the earth, and you will never soar on wings through the endless skies. All creatures must find their own places."

As Owl looked at Wolf, she saw that he cast his eyes to the earth as it passed beneath them. They would always remain two creatures of the darkness, seeing two different nights before them. Still they understood their duty to their traveler was not complete.

Wolf spoke at last, "I can't see through your eyes, Owl. You are able to leave the earth far behind while I see darkness in the forest on all sides. But together we want the same thing, a world of understanding for Kumi. Together we have shown him each of our worlds, all the beauty and danger of the long, dark night. We have given him a gift. I have no doubt he will use it well."

Owl sighed as she looked down. The mountain appeared beneath her, and she began her slow descent. With quiet power she brought them to the mountaintop. They stepped onto the snow-covered path as they began their final journey together.

CHAPTER 12

From a Distant Land

The cold winds of the north chilled Kumi as the night travelers continued their journey. He buried himself deep in Wolf's heavy fur, watching his friend's hot breath swirl around them as they walked along the path to the village below.

Kumi stood among the people of the northern village, straight and proud with his companions of the long night's journey.

He spoke with strength, "I am Kumi, and I have come to learn."

A young child came forward and took his hand. Together they walked to a lodge at the edge of the dark village. Kumi bent down to enter and found many were seated within the circle to greet him.

"I have traveled a long way this night," he told the gathering. "I have come to find the answers to many questions. Is there one among you willing to share your wisdom with a stranger?"

He watched as one by one the quiet eyes looked around in the firelight. Then, as if by some unspoken words, each one of the shadowed faces looked to a figure dozing in the background. The small boy who had led Kumi to the gathering walked quietly to the figure and spoke.

"Auntie, a stranger has come. Wolf and Owl have brought him from far away to learn and to hear what you alone can share."

The figure sat up, refreshed from her short slumber to gaze into the darkness of the lodge.

"Come closer. I must look into your eyes in order to see into your heart."

Kumi approached and then stopped, suddenly frightened. The woman gazed at him with eyes as blue and as pale as the ice that drifted across the northern seas.

"Who are you?" he asked. "Where have you come from?"

She stood up slowly, unfolding her long legs until she stood taller than anyone in the lodge. Her hair was the color of the sun, and she smiled with pleasure at the guest who had arrived so unexpectedly.

"Your people have walked the earth for many generations, Kumi. You have a family and a village where you have been protected and loved. But the world is a large and wonderful place, and there are others who walk upon it. There are many like you and many far different. You must learn, as all those who share the earth must, to walk in balance with all living things.

When you see me, you see someone unlike anyone you have ever known. My appearance seems very strange to you, and that can be a frightening thing. But as you have traveled to this place with Wolf and Owl, you have seen all things can live in harmony. The world grows when we accept and learn from those we do not know or understand. I have come to be with the people so we may share the knowledge each of us has gained."

"Help me to understand," Kumi asked. "Just when I think I know all I need to know, there is more to learn. Will it always be this way? Will I ever have all the answers I seek?"

The pale eyes twinkled as she replied, "Kumi, you will never have all the answers because with each answer, there will be more questions. This is how we learn and grow. Answers are not all there is to knowledge. Questions are the beginning of wisdom, and wisdom brings more questions."

CHAPTER 13

Common Ground

"You have come for a lesson, something to take back to your time. Sit with me and listen as I once sat in your place and listened to the elders. My grandmother taught me many things. One of the most important lessons I will now share with you.

No two creatures are alike, yet we all have a reason and a purpose. I am far different than anyone you have ever known or even imagined. You might think we are too different to understand each other's life. Yet you and I can learn to know one another, can understand each other's joys, and can share each other's tears and sorrows.

Once there was a beautiful, peaceful lake where a single artichoke grew. The artichoke knew he was special, and he was very proud and happy with his place in the world. On the banks of this same lake lived a muskrat. Each evening as the sun began to set the muskrat would walk along the banks of the lake, watching the birds and the insects that flitted across the surface.

One evening he wandered to the edge of the lake where the artichoke stood, proud and straight.

"Who are you?" he asked the artichoke. "You seem quite proud, standing there among the reeds."

The artichoke told the muskrat his name, 'I am from a very large and handsome family. I have relatives all around this area. Who are you? I have never seen you or anyone like you before.'

The muskrat looked at the artichoke and sneered, 'I come from a large family too. But we are busy, and we work hard. We are strong and travel through the water. All you do is stand there in the mud doing nothing.'

The artichoke replied angrily that he had better things to do than swim through dirty water all day and sleep in a mud house at night.

"You are jealous of my beautiful fur and my way of life. I can leave the water at night and clean my fur. You stand in mud all your life, never having excitement or adventure. The only way for you to leave the mud and filth is for men to come and dig you up."

"Perhaps I live my life in the mud by the lake side, but at least I do not smell of musk," the artichoke laughed.

The muskrat stopped for a moment and stared at the artichoke.

"'Sadly, men do not mind my smell. They trap my family so they can take my tail and to make sinew and thread for sewing.'"

The artichoke listened to the muskrat and then replied, 'And the warriors do not mind that I have spent my life in the mud. They pull my relatives from the ground and never even give thanks for our sacrifice. They eat us without taking the time to wash the dirt from our roots.'

The pale eyes gazed at Kumi, who was filled with unasked questions. He sat quietly for several moments, saying nothing as he heard the end of the story.

"There is a message to be learned from the story of the artichoke and the muskrat, Kumi. What have they learned from one another?"

"Auntie, are you trying to tell me that, no matter how different we may be, we face the same worries in our lives? The artichoke and the muskrat each think their world is best, and yet each is in danger from the same enemy."

The sunlit hair fell across her face as she bent over to speak quietly to Kumi, "Our muskrat and artichoke are as different as any two creatures on this earth can possibly be. We are all different in many ways. Our lives may take us in opposite directions. We may eat, sleep, work, and play in ways strange to one another. We will only live in peace when we are all connected to one another, understanding if we do not work together, we may someday destroy each other and the earth, which was a gift from the Creator for our use. Differences are not evil or to be feared, Kumi. They are the colorful patchwork that makes our world the place of beauty it is."

"Why has it become like this?" Kumi was confused by the thoughts shared by the pale lady with the piercing blue eyes. "Have men always been so foolish?"

CHAPTER 14

Turtle Island

"Let me tell you how life came to be calm and kind in this place where you visit us tonight. It was not always this way, Kumi. You are now in a lodge of the Lakota people. The Lakota have learned to share their lives with all the creatures of their world. They have long understood the debt they owe to the Creator for the gifts they have received. They remember a time when the people lost everything, and they now fight to keep their promises to protect their world.

Long ago there had been another world. The people of that world became cruel and unkind to one another. They mistreated the earth and the creatures sharing their world.

The Creator grew angrier and angrier. As his anger grew, he began to sing, and his songs brought the rains. The rains came harder and longer than they ever had. Soon the rains began to cover the earth until, finally, there was a great flood covering the entire first world, killing all the first people. Only the crow, lived and he found himself alone and sad.

Crow begged the Creator for a resting place. Feeling saddened by the flooded world, the Creator decided to make a new world where the people would be kind to one another and respect all living things. He reached into his tobacco pouch, opening the end wide. The loon came out of the bag first. He dove deep into the waters of the flood. He tried to reach the place where he could find mud to bring to the surface, but the waters were too deep. Next came the otter who also tried and failed. Beaver came out of the bag, using his strong tail to help him reach the bottom of the waters. But the water was too deep even for him, and he had to return to the surface in defeat.

The Creator dug deep into his bag and found Turtle. He brought Turtle out and asked him to go to the bottom to bring up earth for the new world. Turtle agreed and sank slowly into the murky water. He was gone for a very long time, and his fellow animals began to weep, for they were sure he had drowned. Suddenly the water on the surface broke, and there was Turtle, caked with mud! The Creator collected the mud from Turtle's back and feet. He spread the mud across the waters so that he and Crow could finally sit and rest. He then reached into his bag and pulled out two eagle feathers. As he waved them across the mud and the water, the land began to grow until there was dry land across the face of the earth.

The earth looked so dry the desolate land he had made saddened the Creator. He began to cry, and soon his tears turned to oceans, crystal-blue lakes and rivers filled with fish. He named the new world Turtle Island to honor the brave Turtle who had provided the mud from which it was formed.

As the Creator pulled the new life from his bag, he remembered how the people had destroyed the first world he had given them. This time he took earth of many different colors to create men and women. He promised them that as long as they honored the gift of this new world, they would live in peace and happiness, but if they forgot his warnings, he would destroy them again."

Kumi sat in silence as the story ended. When he spoke, it was a strong voice, the voice of the honorable man who had grown from the wondering child.

"You have protected this place, and I can see you have all lived as you were instructed. It is time for me to go home and take the teachings back to my own time. I thank you for your lessons and for the guidance you have offered to a weary traveler this night."

"Farewell, Kumi. It is now your turn. As you have been taught, now you must teach others. There are young ones who will come after you. Tell them those things you have learned this night. Tell them how they must learn to live in harmony or their world could cease to be. Tell them of the others, different than themselves yet sharing the same earth. Teach them to honor one another and to protect the gifts the Creator has given them. Return home now and remember."

As he emerged from the lodge, he was struck once again by the chilled night air of the north wind. He looked around and saw his guides, waiting patiently in the shelter of the rocks.

They watched Kumi's approach and saw he had once again grown older with the knowledge he had received. The child they had brought on the long journey had grown old as he had learned.

CHAPTER 15

Home Again

The light was beginning to cross the sky as Kumi's eyes slowly began to flutter and then close. He slept deeply as they three traveled home to the forest clearing. Wolf and Owl set him down on the mossy ground. They looked at Kumi and then at one another.

"Do you see, Wolf? The child has grown on our journey, first with the questions of the young, then with the wisdom of the elders. He has joined them now."

Wolf looked at Kumi. His hair had turned white; his face was kind but appeared to be marked by the passing of many winters.

"We have journeyed long this night, my friend. The child, now grown old, holds the answers to many questions. What he chooses to do with that knowledge is a choice only he can make. We must trust he will share the gifts he has received as the Creator intended."

As the sun climbed higher into the morning sky, Kumi stretched his legs and yawned. Slowly he sat up, looking around the deserted clearing where he had begun his quest so long ago. He was alone, his companions gone with the darkness of the long night.

As he stood his back ached with the stiffness of many years, and he understood. He was Kumi, the grandfather, now. The young child with so many questions was a memory. He had a purpose now and a responsibility. He knew what he must do.

EPILOGUE

"It is so late, Grandfather! I have to get back to the village before the sun sets. May I come back tomorrow to visit with you again? I want to hear more about your journey and the lessons Wolf and Owl shared with you."

Kumi smiled at the young boy. He was remembering a time, so long ago, when he knew very little of the world. He remembered the questions and the long search for understanding.

"You may return any time. You are the reason I am here."

Jumping from where he had been seated, the child darted down the path toward home. He paused, turned, and ran back to the grandfather.

"Grandfather, do you think Wolf and Owl remember the journey as well as you do?"

Kumi nodded, smiling. "Wolf and Owl will always remember."

The boy's short legs pumped quickly as he sprinted through the forest toward the distant sounds of the village. He was getting closer; home was just past the clearing ahead.

He stopped suddenly, hearing a small sound. He looked around in the shadows of the giant trees. There it was again.

Walking carefully across the mossy forest floor the boy came to the base of the gnarled tree where he had learned to climb just last summer. Lying on the ground, almost hidden from his view, rested a tiny sparrow. He could see the little bird's heart beating in her chest. She looked frightened, but she did not move.

"Oh, you've been hurt." His voice was filled with concern. He bent over and gently picked up the tiny bird. "I know you can't tell me what's wrong, but maybe I can help."

The sparrow looked up at him, trusting his kindness. Then she smiled to herself.

The circle could begin again…

PART 2

The Darkness

PROLOGUE

High in the dark sky, where the old ones wait and guard the memories, Owl awakened from her long sleep, stretched out her great white wings, and began the long flight toward the brightness below.

The sun was beginning to set as Owl flew down from her perch high atop the ancient oak tree. She had seen the movement in the trees and knew he was approaching. She had waited many years, and he had finally returned. Wolf, her dearest friend, was slinking quietly though the shadows.

"Old friend," she called to him, "I have been waiting."

He looked up into the fading light and watched as she glided silently to rest on the rocks where he stood.

"I have waited many years for your call, Owl. I am anxious to hear where our adventure will take us this time."

She smiled. "We have been called to take another young one back to the darkness, at the beginning where she will learn how all of life began. She has a friend who cares deeply for her. He wants her to learn to see in both the darkness and the light. But she can only begin to understand the light once she has learned not to fear the darkness. It's time to meet Joe and Jenny."

CHAPTER 1

Powwow Time

Jenny loved the swirling colors of the powwow. As she pulled her glittered shawl around her shoulders, she thought back to the first time she had come to dance. At just three years old, she had danced with the tiny tots as the drums beat through the summer air. The judge placed a dollar in her hand that day, telling her she was a champion. She still laughed at the memory; they were all champions in the tiny tots.

Since the time of her grandmothers, powwows had remained the same in many ways. There were the traditional men dancers, in their eagle and hawk feather bustles, the grass dancers with their flowing yarn and ribbon, women jingle dancers who made music as they walked across the grass and dirt, beautiful beaded buckskin dresses and eagle wing fans that had been handed down through the generations. This was her place, and this was her history. She had just turned eleven, and although she still loved to hear the stories the grandmothers told of the old times and the old ways, Jenny was not yesterday. She was "now," with her cell phone in her pocket, ready to text message her friends on the other side of the arena. She loved the old stories, but there was no way she would ever have been able to live back then!

Summer weekends were the time to meet with friends, dance through the day and into the night to the beating of the drums, eat fry bread, and giggle about the young male dancers. She especially loved the nights when the glitter and the bells sparkled in the lights that shone from high above the arena. Nothing looked the same at night; there was a feeling of anticipation in the cooling air. More than anything, when Jenny heard the drums, she wanted to dance.

Then she heard the announcer, "Two-step! Ladies' choice!"

She moved quickly as her eyes darted around the arena. There was Joe, her brother's best friend. For years he had teased her, argued with her, and watched over her. He was another brother, just like Jason. Well, maybe not just like Jason. After all, he was Joe.

Jenny had seen him for the first time when she was six. She had tripped over the wires that ran behind the announcer's tent and had fallen hard on the rocks and gravel. She began to cry, huge gulping sobs, as she laid tangled in the wire. The first things she saw were the feet, huge feet, in beaded moccasins.

Then he leaned over and, helping her up, commented, "Taking a trip?"

She looked up into laughing hazel eyes hidden beneath a headdress of hawk and raven feathers.

"What's your name, kiddo?"

"Jenny."

"Are you okay? Where's your family?"

He took her hand and walked with her toward the large vendor's booth where her mom and dad were selling T-shirts.

"Excuse me. Your little acrobat here took a nosedive in the gravel. I think she cut her knee."

Now that she really looked at him, she saw he was about the same age as her brother, Jason. Jason was a pest. He never let her go anywhere with him, he always called her "kid," and he thought he was so hot. Big brothers could be more trouble than they were worth sometimes.

That had been five years ago. It was hard to believe he had only been a little older than she was now. He had seemed so much older. He seemed larger than life all those years ago, and in her eyes, he had never changed. Even after he and her brother became best friends, she always secretly knew he had been her friend first.

He was seventeen now, taller than most of the dancers. And he always waited for her when it was ladies' choice, even if he had to pretend not to see the pretty teenage girls who appeared out of nowhere when the two-step began.

Smiling down at her, Joe reached out, and she grabbed onto his hands as they heard the music beginning. The head dancers began, and they fell in step as the line of dancing couples snaked by them. Jenny looked around at the other couples and couldn't help feeling a little smug. All the older girls glared at her, but she didn't care. When she had been only seven years old, she had asked him one day for a promise.

"What do you want?'

"Just promise."

"Okay, I promise to do whatever you want if I can. How's that?"

She had made him promise she could have the first two-step at every powwow. It had been an easy promise at the time, but as the years went on, he had begun to watch the older girls as they danced around the arena, flirting and smiling at him. They would look for him during grand entry, stand near him as he watched the contests, and dance close by during the intertribal dances when everyone danced together. But he kept his word, and Jenny knew it made her the envy of the circle. She smiled and wished the music would go on all night.

CHAPTER 2

The Darkness

The lights always looked strange at night; it was the way the dust rose from the arena, making it look as though there were smoke rings forming around them in the darkness. As Joe led Jenny through the intricate steps of the dance, she gazed up into those silvery rings. She was startled to see the shadow of the giant bird as it flew quietly into the light.

Joe followed Jenny's gaze and watched as the bird circled the arena. Then he stopped and pointed up.

"Look, Jenny," he said. "The moon's gone. I think it's going to rain."

It almost never rained during powwow season, but the wind had picked up, and he felt the cool breeze that sometimes came just before a summer rain. And where was the full moon that had lit the surrounding hills so clearly only moments before? He was glad they would have shelter under the canopy her parents always had over their booth. He started to guide her toward the edge of the circle when the lights flickered and went dark.

The circle was suddenly plunged into total darkness. All around they heard the dancers laughing and talking, teasing about the darkness as they tried to make their way to their chairs and canopies before the rain came.

Jenny felt the chill air blow across her face, and she held more tightly to Joe's hand. As they made their way through the crowd of dancers, Jenny began to tremble. She had never liked the dark. At eleven years old she still slept with a night-light; the dark seemed too large and too empty to her.

They reached a clearing where Joe knew they were far enough from the crowd not to get stepped on or knocked over if they stopped moving. As he stood there, holding Jenny's shaking hands, the loud laughter began to fade until he heard nothing but the sound of Jenny's frightened breathing.

"What's wrong?" he asked. "It's only a power failure. They'll have it fixed soon."

"I know. I'm just being silly. Please don't tell Jason. He'll tell everyone that I'm a baby."

Joe seemed to be listening to something in the distance.

"I think the guys are building a fire over there. I saw some sparks. Yeah, smell that? The wood must be a little wet. It smells like smoke. You stay right here, and I'll go find a flashlight."

She grabbed his hand more tightly. "Please don't leave me alone. I really hate the dark. I can't even sleep in my own room if the door is closed. Once when we were playing hide and seek, I hid in a closet. There was a crack of light under the door, and it was okay until someone turned the light off. I got real scared. I tried to open the door, and it was stuck. Please don't leave me here alone."

"Jenny, did I ever tell you about my grandmother? Sit down. I have to tell you the story she told me when I was little and afraid of the dark. She told me about her grandmother's grandfather and a trip he took a long time ago. I'll tell it to you, but you have to pay attention because someday you'll have to tell the story to someone else. Deal?"

She sat down close to his side, reached out to shake his hand, and solemnly promised, "Deal."

"Well, Grandma used to tell me stories about the long-ago time of the old ones when our people had lost their homes and their land. Lots of them traveled long distances to live on the reservations. They lost so much: their family, friends, traditions, and language. Some of the people began to forget who they were. They couldn't hunt or travel where they wanted. They ate food they had never known and wore strange clothes.

But sometimes, on the darkest nights, when there was no moon to light the way, they would sneak off into the woods to tell the old stories to the young children so they would remember the times that were gone. They were told to listen with their ears and their hearts because these stories had to be told over and over for at least seven generations.

Victor was my grandma's grandfather. He was so young when the changes started he might have forgotten the ways, but on those dark nights, he was one of the ones who sat in the forest and listened all night. Of all the stories he knew he had to remember, the most important to him was the story of his own grandfather, Kumi.

Kumi had been really young when he traveled a long way one night to go into the past with his guides, a wolf and an owl. Wolf and Owl had shown him how important it was to learn to see through the darkness. When he learned to stop being afraid of the darkness, Kumi was able to learn the lessons his guides were trying to share. They wanted him to know how men had lost their connection to the earth. When it was Victor's time to learn these lessons, he wasn't able to leave the reservation, so he had to travel through Kumi's memories to learn the old ways."

Jenny had stopped trembling and was listening intently. The whole thing sounded confusing, but she trusted Joe. She always felt safe with him and knew that he wanted her to learn something from the story he was telling.

"So...," she began. "How did he stop being afraid of the dark?"

"By learning we all come from the darkness. It was our first home, a long time ago. Remember, in the beginning, there was nothing but darkness, and everything you see around you now began in the dark. If we started in the dark, then we should feel at home in it, don't you think?"

She sat quietly, turning the things he had said over in her mind. He made it sound reasonable, but she knew she'd still want her night-light when she went to bed after the powwow.

CHAPTER 3

The Return of Wolf and Owl

"Oh, look. The fire is finally going. Let's go over where it's light." Joe laughed. "You didn't hear a word I said, did you? You're way too young to need hearing aids!"

They walked slowly to the middle of the circle where the fire was blazing brightly. Joe looked around.

"Where is everyone?"

The arena was empty. The bright canopies and vendors tents were gone; the drums were silent. There were no sounds drifting from the parking lot or the streets surrounding the powwow grounds. There was only silence and the dancing red-and-orange flames.

Jenny looked up at Joe, fear clouding her huge brown eyes. He saw the tears beginning to glisten and watched as one silently slid down her freckled cheek. He held tightly to her hand as they walked closer to the fire.

It was then he saw them. There, on the northern edge of the circle, he saw the old man and the snowy owl that sat perched on his arm. He turned and looked to the other side of the arena. To the south he saw others. And he began to understand. He tapped Jenny on the shoulder and pointed east and then west. At each direction he saw the grandfathers, and he knew it was her time, Jenny's time. He knelt beside her.

"Jenny, I think they have come here for you. It must be your turn. I think they are here to teach you just the way they taught

Kumi all those years ago. Maybe they are here to teach you to understand the things that scare you, like the dark.

Look, the grandfather from the north brought a snowy owl. Don't be afraid of the owl. I know you have been told the owl is the messenger of death. But owls also remind us death is part of life. I was told death should never be feared, but it should be respected. Owls are very wise. They know where life began because they can see through the darkness to the beginning.

I can't go with you, Jenny, but I'll wait as long as it takes for you to come back. They're here for you, not for me."

She nodded, walked slowly into the shadows, and disappeared from sight.

CHAPTER 4

Jenny: The Journey Begins

It was too dark. Jenny hated the darkness; it really did scare her. No matter how hard you tried to see something, all you could see was more darkness. She would never learn from this. She wanted to go home.

"Why am I here? Why me?"

The grandfather reached out and touched her head. Slowly her eyes began to focus, and she could see shadows in the darkness. She looked up at the old man and saw his eyes were kind. The owl still sat perched on his arm. It cocked its head and spoke gently.

"I am Owl. I have lived through many lifetimes. I have lived through your lifetime, your parents', and their parents' before them. I have seen the new times and the old times. I have seen the light while living in darkness. We are here to teach you that to live in the darkness does not mean you cannot see. It means you see things differently. We are going back to the beginning of time, when no one feared the darkness because they knew nothing else. Remember, Jenny, everyone fears what they do not know. If you had never known the light, you would fear it as you now fear the dark."

The grandfather took her hand, and Jenny followed as he led her through the misty shadows back toward the beginning of time.

"As you travel this night, you will see light and dark are not the same for all people. You will learn darkness can be more than a lack of light. Lack of understanding or knowledge can be a type of darkness as well. Fear is a darkness in your mind and in your heart.

But when you understand this, you will come to understand a great truth. You will learn the dark and the light are brothers.

To the north, all was dark in the beginning. Some say it was into this darkness the raven was born. He was alone, weak, and frightened. He didn't know where he was or even what he was. He walked alone through the darkness. He reached out with his wings to feel the trees and the plants as he traveled through the darkness. As he touched the plants and rocks of the darkness, he began to understand. He was Raven, the creator of life. As he walked on, he grew stronger. His strength continued to grow, and soon he found he could fly. He stretched out his wings and soared high out of the darkness into a new place. In this place there was nothing, and Raven knew it was the place where he would put the life he was to create. He called this new place, earth. He remembered the trees he had felt in the darkness and knew the earth must have plants too.

One day as Raven flew over his new earth, he saw a giant plant. It was huge, larger than anything other than the trees. It looked like a peapod. He flew down closer to look and saw it was beginning to open. As the pod burst open, a man stepped out, the first man. Raven was very fond of this new man and created the caribou and the reindeer for him. Raven taught the man to hunt so that he would be able to feed himself. When Raven saw the man, he had created was a good man who honored and respected the other life he had put on the earth he wanted to do more. So he created a woman as his companion. He taught them to make all the things they would need for a good life, homes to live in, and clothing to wear. Raven soon planted more pods, and other men began to fill the earth he had created. His people became parents and grandparents, and their descendants still honor the gifts he provided to this day.

Raven came into the world of light, bringing the lessons he had learned in the darkness. He did not leave the darkness until he understood who he was and what he must do. The light did not show the way from the darkness. It was the dark that led him to the light."

CHAPTER 5

Facing Fear

The grandfather smiled down at Jenny.

He placed his hand gently on her head and asked, "Why you, Jenny? Why have I brought you into this darkness? Raven came into darkness and created his own light from what he found as he learned to make his way through the world as it was. I have no answers, Jenny, only another question. Can you learn to find your way through the darkness to the place where you will finally see and understand? This is a choice only you are able to make."

As her eyes tried once again to focus in the darkness surrounding her, Jenny thought about the words the grandfather had spoken. She thought back to her home, her family, her brother waiting to tease her and laugh at her fears and worries.

"Grandfather, my brother says girls are sissies. He tells me girls are weak and can't do all the things that boys can do. Is he right? Are girls weak? Is that why I am always so scared?"

"Fear is not a bad thing, Jenny. Fear tells us that something doesn't feel as it should. A newborn baby fears nothing. He has not learned those things awaiting the careless or the foolish. Fear is what we learn from what we know and, remember this, from what we don't know. We fear what 'might' be out there far more than we fear what we 'know' is out there.

Do you have more fears because you are a girl? Perhaps. But that is because the world has told you what you must fear, and you have learned to believe. But, Jenny, the darkness should never be the thing you fear. The dark is as much a gift as the light, for without it, there would be no balance in life.

From the beginning of time, women have created life. High up in the cold lands of the north, the people have come to honor the women who fight to ensure the future of this world. Even back in the beginning of this land, when the giants still lived, there was a girl child born whose strength still helps to sustain the people.

Sedna was born to the giants who lived there during that long-ago time. Each day the sun faded more quickly into the cold sky, growing weaker with each day break. But as the sun grew weaker, Sedna grew stronger until she was more powerful than any of the giants in the land. She continued to grow, eating all the food in the village and looking for more.

The people knew they would all die if they allowed Sedna to continue to live in the village. With a great struggle, the men bundled Sedna up in a blanket and carried her to a canoe. It was very dark as they paddled out to sea in the shadowed moonlight. When they reached the middle of the ocean, they pushed the girl overboard into the icy waters.

This may sound cruel, Jenny, but the men feared if this girl lived, all of them would surely starve and die. Fear of the unknown drove them to this terrible moment.

As they paddled back to shore, the boat began to shake, and the men feared they were going to drown in the cold, dark water. And then they saw Sedna had begun to change, each of her fingers and toes turning into a creature of the sea. One became of whale, then a salmon, then a walrus, and another became a seal. Soon the seas were filled with amazing and wonderful creatures Sedna created for the people.

Slowly she drifted to the ocean floor, where her new creations built her an underwater home. She stays there still, bringing food and life to the people above during the cold, hard winters when nothing will grow in the icy northern land."

Jenny looked into the darkness and could now pick out the shadows that surrounded them as the grandfather told his story. She looked up into his deep, dark eyes and smiled tentatively.

"Grandfather, the men were more afraid of her strength than she was of the dark, cold sea. They left her there to save themselves, but in the end, she saved them all. Grandfather, she was stronger than all of them, wasn't she?"

"Child, each day we all face challenges that frighten us. Neither men nor women can say they are braver or stronger than the other. Each challenge we face, each darkness we conquer, takes us closer to understanding the balance of light and dark. Just as neither light nor dark is more powerful, we must say the same for men and women. You have great strengths yet to surface. They are hidden deep in your heart, and they will show themselves when it is your time."

CHAPTER 6

Joe's Turn

Joe settled on the dirt, gazing into the fire as he watched Jenny walk into the dark night. He laid back, looking up into the sky, straining to see even the smallest star in the inky blackness. He wasn't sure how long he had been there when he heard a rustling in the trees that surrounded the fire-lit arena. Sitting up, he noticed the two figures walking slowly from the shadows. He could see they weren't Jenny and the old man, but who were they? The two shadows approached the fire, and in the glow of the flames, they became Wolf and Owl.

"Hello, Joe. We have come for you too. We heard you telling Jenny it was her turn, but you must know this is your time as well. Jenny has gone with the grandfather to learn what was. Your lesson is more complicated. You were chosen long ago to learn one thing, one very important lesson. Jenny will learn what was, and still others will come to understand what could be. You were chosen by the old ones to learn what should be. Do you understand the difference?" Owl spoke carefully, wanting to be certain the young man from this new time was able to hear the message they brought from long ago.

Joe looked at the visitors: the wise Owl, with her all-seeing eyes; and Wolf, with his powerful presence. He did not speak but sat, thinking, *What should be... Can anyone ever know for sure what should be?*

He stood up, and Owl flew to perch on his shoulder.

"You are the one, Joe. Long ago, your great-grandfather and his before him told us you would come. They asked that we guide you.

70

You will not travel to the four directions. You have learned those ways from childhood. We are here to guide you in your own direction. We will journey this night to your people and their past. Tonight as Jenny learns how all of life began, how the darkness is a gift from the Creator, and how to face her fears, you will learn how your life began. She will travel into the unknown, while we will travel to the sacred mountains and prairies of your past."

Wolf had stood silently, observing the young man with great interest.

Now he spoke, "You are born of great people. If you are to know what should be, you must know how these people came to walk this earth. You must know the ways of long ago so you may use that knowledge to bring about what should be tomorrow."

"But I promised Jenny I would wait for her. She'll be scared if she comes back and I'm gone. I haven't broken a promise to her since she was a little kid. I can't start now." Joe thought of Jenny, her wide eyes pleading with him to stay where he was, and knew breaking a promise was hardly the way to begin a journey to learn respect.

His guides looked at one another and smiled knowingly.

"You see, Wolf. I told you he would say that. I know these young ones we choose so well. He made a promise, and he will honor that promise."

"Joe, Jenny's journey this night will take her to the far corners of time and space. Each time she returns, she will know you are here, for a piece of your spirit will not leave this place where you have given your word. But you will travel with us in your own direction with that part of your spirit that knows there is much to learn. It is your time now. Place your hand on Wolf's head, and our journey will begin."

The wind began to blow, and the dark clouds billowed around the travelers. Joe held tightly to Wolf's soft fur while feeling the powerful muscles that rippled beneath its surface. *He is really strong*, he thought. *He doesn't have to act tough. He knows who he is and it shows. You've got to respect that.* Joe thought of the guys he knew at school. You had to be a football player, a wrestler, whatever, just to get by. *It shouldn't be that way*, he thought.

71

Owl smiled as she listened to his thoughts. *He is already beginning to see what shouldn't be. It is only a few steps from there until he understands what should be.* It was going to be an interesting journey.

CHAPTER 7

Trust

In the distance Jenny could see a faint glow. Focusing on the glow, she held the grandfather's hand and began walking to the light. As the light began to grow brighter, she saw him. Joe stood patiently in the firelight, just as he had promised. She reached out her hand, and Joe drew her back into the warmth of the fire.

"Thank you, Grandfather," said Joe, "for taking care of my little sister. She's important to me, and I want her to learn all she can tonight."

The old man smiled, turned, and wordlessly returned to his seat at the northern edge of the circle.

"Well, tell me what you learned." Joe looked at Jenny with interest.

"Well, I learned Jason is wrong. I am not a sissy. It just isn't my time yet."

Joe laughed. "Well, that's as good a way to start this night as any. You know, it's okay to be afraid of things. Everybody's afraid of something. My dad gets scared on Ferris wheels, and my mom hates mice. But they are the bravest people I know. Being scared is not a bad thing. Letting fear rule your life is."

Jenny laughed. "Jason's scared of snakes. He thinks nobody knows, but his friend has a corn snake, and it freaks him out!"

As they stood talking, Joe could feel the breeze beginning to blow gently from the east. He watched as Jenny's hair blew across her eyes, and he reached out to smooth it back.

"Your journey has only started. I see your next guide waiting. It's time, kiddo."

"Please come with me." Her eyes were pleading. "It was really dark there. I promise I'll listen, but it would be easier if you were there too."

"I know. But don't you see? That's the reason I can't go with you. This isn't supposed to be easy. This is your journey, Jenny. I'll be here when you come back. Have I ever broken a promise to you?" he asked.

Together they walked east, to the old man seated on a gnarled tree stump. His hand rested lightly on the back of a great gray wolf waiting patiently at his side. Joe reached out to stroke the wolf's head and then looked down at the elderly man.

"Grandfather, this is Jenny. Please watch over her while she travels with you tonight."

Jenny looked at the wolf uneasily and stepped closer to Joe. He laughed softly.

"My great-grandfather told about the wolf that guided Kumi long ago. The wolf brought strength and protection that time. Remember the wolf watches for danger during the long nights and sees where others can't. You will be safe with him, Jenny."

The grandfather spoke quietly, "Child, as the wolf knows he must care for his pack, each of us must learn to care for one another. Each of us must learn we are called to share our strength with those who are weaker, just as the wolf shares his strength with his family.

"Jenny, this wolf is your friend. He has waited to teach you about the darkness, and he knows you will follow him into the night he and his people respect. He will keep us safe as we journey to an unknown place and time."

Jenny looked back over her shoulder at Joe. Her eyes reminded him of her trust and his promise.

"I'll be right here, Jenny," he said, knowing the piece of his spirit he had left for her would always honor that promise, even as another part of him would soar through the night on his own journey of discovery.

CHAPTER 8

Joe: Going Home

Joe felt the sudden jolt of the land beneath his feet as he and his guides came to rest next to a warm fire. He looked around the circle to the kind faces of the men and women who sat waiting for his arrival.

"Welcome, old friends," an old man with gnarled hands and leathery skin greeted Wolf and Owl.

"Grandfather, this is Joe. We have brought him to meet his past, for that way, he will come to understand who he is. We have been waiting for him a long time. He is the one." Owl looked very serious as she spoke.

"Oh, so he is the one. We were beginning to wonder if he would really come. Are you sure?"

"Oh, yes. He asks the questions he needs to ask. And he listens, Grandfather. It seems so few of the young ones listen today."

"Joe, we have known for many generations that you would come to learn what should be. But before you can know these things, you must know yourself and your people. Have you ever wondered where your life began?"

Joe looked down at his feet, wondering how to answer this strange question. What should he say? "I know where my life began. It began in the hospital where I was born." Or maybe he should say, "My life started the first time I danced," or "the first time I played football," or "when my parents got married." But he realized he had no idea what the right answer could be, so he said nothing.

"Sit down, Joe. I will tell you as it has been told since the beginning of time. Our people are the people of the Plains. There are many stories told by the old ones of long ago. They are my stories and my father's and Grandfather's before him. They are your stories and those of your mother and grandmother before her. They are the stories of very long ago and not so very long ago. But more important, they are also the stories of tomorrow, for that is when you will tell them."

The old man's face softened as he spoke. He had a message he knew he must give to this young man. He had to find the story that would help guide Joe to the place he needed to go this night.

"Joe," the old man began, "do you know how large the prairies are? Do you know they begin far to the south and go north to the foot of the high mountains? Do you know that across these plains and prairies brave people have fought and died to hold onto the truth of their past and the promise of a better future? Do you know the spirits of your people chose this land to be your home?"

Joe nodded, knowing this was the time to listen in silence. He could hear the grandfather's voice in his heart as well as his ears and knew the lesson he would learn tonight could change him forever.

CHAPTER 9

Joe: The First Grandfathers

"Long ago your grandmother's people were only a thought in the mind of the Creator. All were spirits, with no home, no land to call their own. The spirits searched for a place to settle. Many traveled to the sun. They thought it would be a warm and beautiful place to begin creation. But the sun was so hot nothing could live there. The spirits continued their search and found earth.

Earth seemed like a good spot until they tried to find a place to rest. The earth was covered with the great waters. There was no dry land where life could begin.

The spirits were sad. They had thought earth was going to be their home. But the waters made that impossible, and they prepared to continue their search.

Suddenly, out of the waters of the earth, there came a huge, glowing rock, burning hot and flowing across the waters. As it cooled, it became dry land, a place where the spirits could rest and begin life. Clouds of steam formed over the land, and the gentle rain soon began to fall upon the barren rocks. Plants and trees began to form. The burning rocks were the first beings. They were to become your first grandfathers. Remember to respect the rocks, Joe. They are your reminders of the beginnings of your people. Each time you see the water fall upon the rocks in the sweat lodge, you must remember that moment of creation when the spirits of the first people found their home."

CHAPTER 10

Jenny in the East

"Jenny, I told you the wolf knows he must care for his pack. His pack is his family, and there are both weak and strong in any pack. If the strong turn their backs on the weaker members of the pack, none will survive. We each make choices every day. We hope we make more good choices than poor ones, but that will depend on how we choose. Do we choose with pride alone, thinking only of ourselves? Do we choose with our hearts, thinking of those we must protect?

All the world is a balance, Jenny. Night and day, dark and light, right and wrong. You cannot understand one without understanding the other. You fear the dark without the light. The shadows frighten you when you cannot see beyond them. You must also understand human beings can choose poorly when they do not take the time to look at both sides of each line that is drawn in life.

Sometimes the dark of the night can bring great gifts, but only to those who look through the night and choose wisely with their hearts. They cannot choose with their minds or their desires, for greed and pride can do terrible things to man.

Long ago four warriors began a long journey through the darkness, looking for ways to make this earth a better place for their people. They left their homes with good thoughts and plans for the future. At the end of their travels, they met with a great and powerful grandfather who knew the ways of men. He knew in each of us there is a balance of good and evil, just as in this world there is a balance of light and dark. Where the world cannot survive without light and dark, man must choose between good and evil.

The grandfather's time was short before he needed to return to his home, a magical place hidden in the mists of time and space where men cannot travel as long as they are tied to the world of mortals.

'Each of you will be granted one gift, one wish. Think carefully and choose wisely as this gift carries more power than you know,' the grandfather explained. He then handed each of them a bundle, carefully wrapped and tied with strong vines. 'Think as you travel to your homes. Then you may choose. Open your bundle, and your wish will be granted. This gift can change your world. Think before you speak your words, for they will bind your choice.'

With these words, the grandfather turned and walked to the water's edge. Glancing once over his shoulder, he waved, stepped into his canoe, and began to paddle into the mists. Soon he was out of sight, but his words remained in the ears of the warriors: 'This gift can change your world.'"

Jenny listened intently. "You could make the world such a wonderful place with the right choices. They were really lucky! I can't imagine what I would say. There are too many choices."

"Ah, that is what you would think, isn't it? But, Jenny, sometimes men are careless and thoughtless when they have important decisions to make. Sometimes they choose with their pride instead of their hearts. The men forgot they had to accept the balance in themselves just as we have to accept the balance of the light and dark in our world.

They did not stop to weigh the good they could do for many against the power they sought for themselves. Three of the men couldn't wait until they reached their homes to open the bundles. The thoughts of their own power overtook them. Sadly, they did not remember we are all related, we must work together, or we will never reach the end of our journey with honor.

The first man thought to himself, *If I were bigger and taller than everyone else, I could be more powerful, and I would be chief, and all would obey me.* So the man wished this to be so.

'I wish to be bigger and taller than all others.'

He opened his bundle, tearing at the vines that held the wrapping in place. Suddenly he was turned into the tallest tree in the forest.

The next man, walking on ahead to the river, never saw what became of his traveling companion. He was deep in his own thoughts of power and had decided what his wish would be.

'If I live longer than anyone else, I will become more powerful and wiser than all men.' Opening his bundle, he asked, 'I wish never to die.' As he spoke the words, he was changed into a stone.

The third man watched as his companion turned into a stone by the river's edge. Frightened, he looked for the other travelers. Peering through the trees, he saw the fourth man approach.

'Are you alone?'

'Yes, one of our friends is now a tree in the forest and the other has become a stone.'

The third man thought carefully. *I will not ask to become anything other than what I am. No one will ever wonder if I am a tree or a stone. I will remain myself.* He got into his canoe and began to paddle down the river towards home.

But as he paddled, he began to think, *I can remain myself, but I can become a rich man, and that will make me more powerful than anyone else.* So, opening his bundle, he asked to have more possessions and riches than anyone else in the world. His wish was granted instantly. Little by little his canoe began to fill with treasures of all kinds until his canoe, overflowing with his possessions, began to sink into the river. Soon he was being covered by all he now owned, and at last, he was buried beneath his riches at the bottom of the river and drown.

The fourth man was younger, yet wiser, than his companions. He had thought carefully as he watched his friends lose their way, and their lives, to their greed. He had known what his wish would be from the beginning and waited until he was safely home in his own lodge before making his choice. He had traveled through the darkness and knew he had learned from the mistakes of his companions. He sat alone by his fire until a faint light crept across the land.

The young man closed his eyes and wished for a better life for his people. He wished for them to prosper and be strong and healthy and lead good lives. With this, he opened his bundle. He looked inside and found…nothing. And then he knew. The wishes he had for his people would be fulfilled by sharing his own heart with them. He would teach them to work together, trust one another, and care for each other. The gift was within each of them, not inside the bundle."

The old man sat quietly, his tale complete. He knew he could not hurry or explain. Jenny must come to understand the message in her own time. Her eyes focused on the wise grandfather as her thoughts flew back in time to join the traveling warriors as they made their wishes. A spark lit her dark-brown eyes as she smiled at him.

"I am only one person, Grandfather. I'm just me. Sometimes I make decisions because it's easy or because everyone else is doing something. Is that like making decisions in the dark? Is that what happened to the warriors? They didn't think about anything but right now, this minute, what would make them rich and powerful. My mother always tells me to be careful what I wish for because I might get it. She always says to 'sleep on it.' That's like seeing it in the nighttime and the daylight."

CHAPTER 11

Joe: Walking in Two Worlds

"You are a child of the Great Plains, Joe. This is true, it is what you know. But there is more to your story, Joe, more to who you are. Your journey to knowing what should be cannot end until you have come to understand yourself. Then you will know, then you will be ready.

Joe picked up a handful of dry twigs and leaves and threw them onto the dying embers of the fire before them. The glow deepened, and the flames once again danced to life. The mist had chilled the summer breeze. and his clothes were still damp from the rain.

As Joe sat, warming himself by the fire, he sensed someone watching him from across the flames. Looking up, he was startled to see a woman who was clearly from another time and place. Her bright-green eyes smiled warmly as she shook out her curls, the color of new pennies in the sun.

"Hello, Joe, my name is Sarah. I'm certain you are surprised to be seeing someone looking like me on your journey. But I am some-one you must come to know if you truly want to know yourself."

Where had he heard a voice like that before? His mind turned over and over, and then suddenly he remembered. The Highland Games! Sure, that was it. His mom had dragged him to them a few years back. It had been fun, he had told Jason, kind of like a Scottish powwow.

"Joe, Jenny has gone to learn that, without the darkness, you cannot understand the light. Just as she must learn each is half of one greater whole, so must you. It was your grandmother who put the copper in your skin, but you must now come to understand your grandfather, for it was he who put the emeralds in your eyes. You are born of each of them, and just as light and dark make up the day, the copper and the emerald make you who you are.

There are those who say you must choose your path. You cannot be of two worlds. But you are, Joe. Your heart may live here on the prairies of your grandmother, but your spirit also belongs to your grandfather's highlands far across the ocean. You are of two people. You do not have to choose. It was chosen for you long ago. You are now walking the paths others placed before you."

He looked at her, a puzzled look on his face. Born of two people? Sure, he knew it was true, but he also knew he had needed to choose a path when he was younger than Jenny. And he had chosen his native roots. He was a child of the prairies and the mountains.

"I know all about my grandfather's people. They came from Scotland hundreds of years ago. But that doesn't have anything to do with me. I have been Indian all my life. I've never been Scottish, and I am not about to start now."

She smiled at him, shaking her head. "Joe, you have been Indian all your life. But you have been a Scot all your life as well. It doesn't make you less of who you are. It makes you more. Not knowing who you are doesn't change the fact you are born of two great tribes. Did you know you are of tribal people on each side of the great ocean?

You see, the Celtic people of long ago formed their lives and families around their tribes and clans just as the Indian people of the Americas were doing.

The Highland clans were a proud people, generous and kind, yet fiercely protective of their glens and mountains. Each moor, with its peat bogs, murky waters, bracken and purple heather, was as precious to them as the mountains and plains of the great west were to your grandmother's people.

Follow me, Joe. I want to show you what can happen to those who feel they must choose one world when they are truly born as a part of two."

As she reached her hand across the fire toward him, Joe could feel himself falling. He held tight as they tumbled into the warmth of the dancing flames. The flames burned bright around them as they twisted and turned through time and space. They landed suddenly, tumbling over and over through the bright green of a gentle hillside. Laughing and shouting, they continued to roll until they came to a sudden stop next to a clear, bubbling creek running through the shade of a tall stand of trees.

CHAPTER 12

Joe: The Selkie

Joe stood up, turned, and offered his hand to the woman with the red curls. She smiled as he helped her to her feet.

"Ah, your mother has raised a gentleman, I see," the woman remarked with a smile.

"She'll tell you it wasn't an easy job," Joe replied.

"Joe, this small creek becomes a river just over this hill. Then as it flows to the west, it grows larger until it reaches the rocks that border the great sea. The rocky coast of your grandfather's land has called the people of the hills and the highlands for generations. They come with small boats, searching for the fish that are the gifts the sea provides."

Joe looked out across the water. The sun was shining brightly, and the mist, which so often crept in from the water, had burned off with the midday heat. He saw the water, lapping easily at the foot of the large rocks jutting up from the deep water. Suddenly, a sleek gray body skimmed across the water and climbed easily up onto the largest of the jagged rocks.

"Look, a seal!" he exclaimed, delighted.

"Yes," the woman replied, "a seal. Or perhaps not. Did you know, Joe, you might be very much like that seal? You see, just as you appear to be of only one world, though we know you are of two, that seal might also be more than she seems to be.

Just as that seal may be caught between two lives, you are caught between two as well. It's a sad story, but one that bears telling at this time.

There are creatures here, on this side of the great water, who belong to the world of man and the world of that very seal you stand watching. These creatures are of the land and of the sea. They cannot be happy when they must choose only one of these worlds because each world will call to them when they are living in the other."

Joe looked away from the seal and into the green eyes that had suddenly become so serious.

He spoke quietly. "Tell me," was all he could say.

She sat down on a large smooth rock and gestured for Joe to sit beside her. He sat, waiting patiently for her to begin.

"Can you walk with two feet, each on a different path going in different directions and still end up in the same place?

The selkie is of two worlds and cannot be truly happy unless she is able to travel between the two lands to which she belongs. When she tries to be only one of her two selves, she saddens and dies. My story will show how those she loves and who love her try to trap her on land. She knows she must escape in order to serve the other half of her soul.

I will tell you the story of these sad folks because theirs is the story of all who try to choose what is not theirs to choose. Do you understand what I am telling you, Joe?"

"No, I'm sorry. I have no idea what you are talking about."

"Listen, my boy. I think you will begin to see what it is you are needing to know.

There was a man with a fine and prosperous farm who lived not far from the seaside. He was strong and handsome, and all the young maidens in the nearby villages set their sights on marrying this eligible, young man. No matter what they did, he had no interest in them. He was waiting for someone, someone special, someone he knew would come along someday.

The young girls tried so hard soon they became angry with the young farmer. They laughed at him and made fun of him. Soon they began calling him names, and they refused to look at him or speak to him.

They did not bother him with their cruel words because he knew one day he would find the one he waited for, and nothing would keep him from making her his own.

Each afternoon this man would walk by the sea, looking out and dreaming of his true love who would come one day. One afternoon as the sun made its trip across the sky, he walked quietly to the shaded place where the jagged rocks jutted out above the wild, breaking waves.

Now, there are selkie-folk who live out and about the rocks of the wild Scottish shores. Ah, I can tell by your face you have never before heard of the selkie-folk, have you?"

Joe shook his head and looked at her in confusion. What was she talking about?

"Joe, there are people in this world who are just like you, and there are people in this world who are nothing like you. There are people who are just what they seem to be and others who are far more than you can begin to imagine they are. The selkie-folk are those who travel between two worlds. They live as you do, walking on this earth, speaking as you speak, sleeping in warm beds at night, tending their families and their homes. But they have another side, a secret life that they must accept, or they will wither and die of the greatest sorrow."

"What is their secret?"

"In the gray of the early morning, the selkie-folk don their other skin, the secret skin that takes them to another world. Joe, the selkie-folk are seals. They frolic in the waves, eating fish and basking on the rocks that dot the coastline. As the afternoon sun rises in the sky, they shed their sealskins and enjoy the warmth of the afternoons on the shore. They are of two worlds, Joe, each as important as the other. Without both, they can only live a half-life, and that half-life can never bring them joy.

So this afternoon, as the young farmer spied upon the gentle selkie-folk, he saw that their enchanted sealskins had been thrown carelessly upon the sand and rocks. Slowly he began to creep closer to them. His eyes fell upon the most beautiful of all the seal maidens, and he knew what he needed to do.

He had found her, that someone for whom he had waited so long. He could not allow her to escape back to the sea. He jumped up and ran as fast as his feet would take him to where the selkies lay, basking in the sun. The selkies cried out as they grabbed their skins and raced back to the safety of the sea. But the farmer was quicker, and he had managed to grab the last sealskin. It was the skin of the beautiful seal maiden he knew must be his wife. Although he saw how sad she looked, he knew she would grow to love him and the life they would share.

He walked toward his home, carrying his prize. He heard her sorrowful cries behind him and knew she would follow where he led as long as he carried her treasured sealskin. He saw the tears flowing down her cheeks, but he continued to walk toward his home. He felt great sorrow for her but knew he could make her forget that other half of herself if she would only allow him to care for her. She was the one he had waited for, and no tears would make him let her go.

Over time the selkie-maiden grew weary of asking for her skin back, and she agreed to marry the farmer. He loved her dearly and was kind and generous. She knew she could never leave where he was, for he had hidden her other self, and to leave would be to lose the other part of who she was.

So they were together for many years. She was a good wife, bearing him many children, making a good home for all of them, and smiling as she went about her chores. To all who knew them, they seemed a happy and devoted couple.

Yet the selkie-maiden never forgot who she was, and she yearned each day to find the other half of herself, for none of us can be truly happy until we are whole.

One day the farmer and his sons went fishing, leaving the selkie-wife home with her daughters. She sent her daughters out the collect berries from the bushes that grew wild on the hillsides. She was home alone, with only her youngest daughter who had a fever and cough. As the little one sat by the fire, she noticed her mother searching the house, every corner and bin.

'What do you look for, Mother? You seem so serious.'

'Ah, my child. I am looking for a lovely, soft skin I would wrap around you to make you warm and comfortable. It is a special skin that will help you to feel much better, but I don't know where your father has put it.'

'Oh mother, I know where it is! One day, while you were all outside and Father thought I was napping, I saw him take a pretty skin down from where it is hidden in the eaves above the bed. He looked at it as if he hated it, but it was so pretty I have never understood why. Then he put it back, and I have never seen it again.'

In her great excitement the selkie-wife began to cry. She went to the bedroom, and finding her treasured skin, she raced out of the house toward to crashing sea and her long-lost seal family.

Her husband and sons, returning from their day at sea, saw her as she began to swim away into the dark waves.

They cried out for her to return to them. She swam near them and looked sadly into their grieving eyes.

'Do you not see I am not only that which you have allowed me to be? Do you not understand I have been only half of myself for all these years? If you had only embraced all that I am, then I would have been happy to stay with you forever. I must leave now because I must search for that which I lost so many years ago."

CHAPTER 13

Joe: Understanding

"They never saw her again, Joe. She lost her family on the land because they could not accept all that she was. Now you have heard their sad story, Joe, so I need to ask you what you have learned from it."

Joe sat, looking out over the dark sea. The waves beat against the rocks as they had for thousands of years. Far in the distance he heard a roll of thunder, telling him the rain was soon to follow. As lightning lit up the dark sky where it met the sea, he looked back to the woman who had brought him to the distant land.

His eyes glistened with tears of sadness—sadness for the selkie, her children, the husband who had never understood her needs, and the seal family that had lost her for so long.

"He never accepted she was born of two worlds, and each of those worlds needed to hold her and let her go at the same time. She tried to be one person when she was two people. She never chose to be human, and she never chose to be seal. She was selkie. She was both."

He stopped suddenly, a light shining in his hazel eyes.

"That's it! I'm a selkie!"

She laughed, "Well, not exactly, but I think you understand. You are two people, boy. You are Indian, be proud of who your grandmother made you. And you are a Scot. Be proud of that part of you your grandfather contributed to the person you have become. If you try to be one while ignoring the other, you will be only half of yourself. In a way, perhaps you are a selkie. Perhaps we are all selkies in some way."

He reached out for her small hand, and he took it in his much larger one. Together they walked into the mist that had begun to gather behind them on the hillside. He smelled the sea and the heather as they walked deeper into the gray swirling clouds that surrounded them.

Far ahead, Joe could see the fog beginning to fade and the light of a distant fire. The woman let go of his hand and smiled at him fondly.

"Joe, you must go back now. You have heard the lesson I was sent to share with you. What you do with that lesson is your choice. You may sit and ponder on what you have heard, or you may toss the message aside, thinking it was nothing more than a story told by the old ones on cold winter nights to entertain the wee ones."

Joe looked into her bright-green eyes one last time.

"I will remember," he promised, "and I will be back. I think this place has more lessons for me to learn."

She smiled, turned, and walked slowly back into the mist that soon enveloped her.

CHAPTER 14

Joe: What Should Be?

Joe looked ahead to the fire burning just beyond the fog and headed toward it. In a moment he was back in the circle where he had left Jenny what seemed like hours ago. Where was she? He hoped she was not sitting in the darkness waiting for him. She would never trust him again.

The circle was quiet as he walked toward the fire. He heard the crackling of the wood and smelled the musky odor that reminded him the wood had been wet when it was lit. He stretched out his hands to the flames as his thought went back to the night's adventures.

The grandfathers were gone; he was alone with only his thoughts to occupy his mind.

"You must learn what should be." That was what they had told him. "What should be…"

He had learned so much about himself, his people, and his past. But what had he learned that was important to everyone? What was there about his past that could help him learn his lesson?

What should be?

His people began here in this land, where the buffalo and the eagle had lived since the beginning of time. This land was a part of him, and he was a part of it. The endless prairies were his home.

This he knew. He also knew this was not what should be; it was a fact.

But as he looked into the flames, thinking he had the answer, he realized with this answer came more questions. Why was it always like that? Just when you figured out what you needed to know, you realized there was more. His thoughts continued to wander.

What had Sarah told him? "Your spirit is also in the Highlands."

He remembered how he had felt, standing in the midst of the heather as he watched the seals play. He tried not to think about how peaceful he had felt, how much at home. How can you feel at home in a place you never knew existed?

Then he remembered something his grandmother had told him when he was very young.

"The blood remembers," she had said. He had never known what she meant until now.

He remembered because his grandfather and his grandfather and his before that had been in that place. They had seen that shore-line and watched the seals as they dove among the waves. It was their place, and because of that, it was Joe's place too.

Suddenly he knew. He grinned as he looked into the fire. He couldn't wait to tell Jenny. Where was she?

CHAPTER 15

Jenny: The Gifts

The darkness of the night was cut by a single flash of lightning and the low rumbling of the accompanying thunder. *Oh great,* she thought. She feared the darkness a lot, but she feared thunder and lightning almost as much. But she had promised Joe, and she knew he trusted her to keep her word. She looked around the arena until she saw them there, where she knew they would be waiting.

There in the shadows cast by the glowing campfire she saw the kindly old grandfather seated in the ground. At his side, on a fallen branch, sat the biggest owl Jenny has ever seen in her life. The great horned owl, strong and majestic, waited for her, and she knew her next steps on her journey were about to begin.

"You fear the storm, Jenny." His voice was deep and soft. "I see it in your face. But you must never fear the thunder and lightning. It helps bring life to the earth. It nourishes the animals and plants. Each storm comes to us as a gift. Without its power, the earth would wither and die.

So many of the things we fear in life have great power. Think how many fear the high mountain passes covered in snow and ice, the thunderous rainstorms, the swirling rapids of the deep rivers. Each of these is a gift from the Creator. When we learn to respect and honor this power, we learn to love those things we once feared so deeply.

Look at my friend, this gentle owl by my side. Native people across this land fear him and his kind. They believe he will bring sadness and death. Remember, without sadness in this world, there is no joy. Without death, would we ever truly live? The owl is not to be feared. His gifts are that he sees what others cannot see, and he knows what few others ever will. He is the wisest of the birds because he has learned to listen to messages of life and spread them to all with ears to hear."

Jenny looked thoughtfully at the beautiful bird seated by the old man's side. He looked at her with such kindness she began to smile.

"Please tell me what you know," she asked.

The owl paused for several moments before speaking, "Jenny, the lesson I have for you to learn is that you, and only you, must earn those things you want in life. You worry because you have fears. We all have fears. But if you want to be brave, be brave. If you want to be kind, be kind. You can choose to share the gifts you have with others, or you can choose not to. You will decide for yourself the person you will become.

Remember, little one, the greatest of our gifts are those we can share with others. But we cannot demand others share their gifts with us, for when we do, we can lose all we hold dear.

In the long-ago time, many generations past, in the traditional land of the people of the plains, there were two young hunters. During a heavy winter snowstorm, they wandered far from their village in search of game to feed their hungry families. As they made their way through the deep drifts among the trees, they saw a beautiful young woman standing before them. They were startled to see her there in the snowy wilderness, but she smiled and told them not to be afraid, for she brought and peace and happiness with her.

'Why are you so far from your village?' she asked.

The older of the two men gazed at her incredible beauty longingly, but finally, the younger of the men was able to speak.

'Our people are hungry, and we have been hunting for game.'

She smiled at him and reached into her heavy robes to show him a bundle she carried. She held it out to him, smiling.

'Take this to your people. Tell your chiefs to gather in the council lodge and wait for me. I come with gifts to share with all of you. Tell them I will be there soon.'

The two men stood as still as the tall grass that surrounded them. She was so beautiful she could not be real. The older of the men was so moved by her beauty he could not stop himself and reached out to touch her. He thought to himself, *I will make her my own, take her to my village, marry her, and she will belong to me forever.* He would not have to share her or her gifts with others. She would be his alone. He was blinded by his greed and his desire.

But as his hand touched hers, she gazed at him in sorrow. Suddenly a great cloud formed around him, and when it finally cleared, he was gone. She knew that his desire to take her gifts for his own cost him everything. He was now lost forever.

The younger man hurried back to his village, telling the story of the woman on the prairie. It sounded impossible. Who was she? Where was her home? Was she even real?

But as the young man had instructed, each of the chiefs dressed in his finest robes and gathered with the others in the council lodge. They sat around the leaping fire, and as the shadows danced upon the walls, a gentle breeze began to blow and the dust swirled around them.

There she was, appearing to them as though in a dream. As the young hunter has told them, she was beautiful, with kind eyes and a gentle presence.

'I have come to share with you my gifts, granted to me by the Creator. I have chosen you of all those in the land. They are truly wonderful gifts. You may choose to keep them for yourself, but to share them with your brothers will make them even more valuable than they already are.'

She reached again into her robes and offered them another bundle, larger than the one she had given the hunter in the woods. She began to open it, and the old chiefs watched in wonder as visions began to dance before their eyes. They saw their people in prayer together, joining hands and welcoming others into their families, dancing together in the morning sun. So many wonderful visions appeared to them as they sat in the fading firelight they had no words to speak to one another or to the lady who shared her gifts of these visions of wonder.

As the visions faded, she walked slowly to the young man she had first met in the woods.

'You have been so kind and have treated me with honor and respect,' she said softly. 'The last gift I give is in your hands. I ask that you guard it now, as it is the most precious gift I give to your people. It is yours to guard, but this too must be shared with others across this land, for it alone will bring peace.'

He opened the bundle, and within he saw a small bowl made of deepest-red clay. It fit snugly into a long wooden holder wrapped carefully with the bowl.

'Share this pipe with others. Offer it to them in peace and friendship. Guard it well and keep it safe. Teach your brothers the gift of peace is the greatest gift of all. We must protect what is ours, guarding our families, our people and our way of life. Sometimes peace will not be possible, but if it is lost, this pipe will help to heal and rebuild those bonds.'

She stayed throughout the winter, teaching them to understand the visions they had seen. She taught the young ones to know they would inherit the ways of their people. As she shared the gifts she had brought, the people grew stronger. And then she knew it was time to go.

In the dim light of the early morning sun she walked across the land she had grown to love. She saw the new grass was beginning to dot the prairie. There were wildflowers peeking through the grass, and the winds held a promise of warm days to follow. The young man she had first met on that snowy day walked with her.

'You have listened well and learned many things. I have shared my gifts. Now you must share them as well. Never let them be forgotten. Each generation must tell the next. Grandfather must tell grandson. Aunties must tell the little ones who visit. Guard the pipe for all time. It will serve your people well as long as you respect its power. Have a good life. Be strong for your people and live in peace.'

He nodded. As she walked toward the horizon, he heard a flock of geese honking their way across the blue sky. He looked up and smiled at their journey. As he looked back to the horizon, she was gone.

He shaded his eyes to try for one last glimpse but saw only a lone white buffalo standing where she had been. The single snow-white creature looked at him for a moment, turned, and walking toward the rising sun, vanished from sight.

He understood. As he turned for home, he thanked the Creator for sending this special visitor who had changed his life forever."

CHAPTER 16

Jenny: Listen to the Silence

The silence was total. Jenny heard no one and saw nothing. She listened for something to let her know she was not alone. Where was Joe? He promised. He never broke a promise, but she didn't see or hear him anywhere.

"Joe?" she whispered. "Are you there?"

"Shh, child," a voice spoke so softly she almost didn't hear it. "Listen to the silence."

Jenny sat down on the hard dirt of the arena. At least she knew where she was. She was back where she started the journey. But where was Joe? As her eyes became accustomed to the darkness, she saw him. He was sitting with the oldest grandfather of all, his hand slowly petting the back of an enormous black wolf. She stood up and began walking slowly toward them.

"Not a sound," said the soft voice.

Was that the wolf talking to her? It was! But why did she need to be so quiet? Was she listening for something? She strained but heard nothing, not the wind, the fire crackling, nothing.

"It is only in the quiet that you will hear your thoughts, the thoughts of others, and the world around you. You will hear what cannot be heard once you learn to listen to the silence. When you cannot see with your eyes, and your mind is silent, your ears will see for you."

Jenny stopped suddenly and shut her eyes. In the silent darkness she let her mind be still and listened to the night. In the distance she heard the cry of a bird, the rustling of leaves. She smelled the damp wood from the fire, and her skin felt a slight warmth, telling her the sun would soon chase the dampness of the night from the sky.

The grandfather walked toward her, smiling.

"Let's go, Jenny. Your journey is nearing its end. Let's find the sunlight before we face one last darkness together."

The night surrounded the travelers, and when the darkness cleared, they were far from the powwow arena once again.

The great black wolf walked carefully across the sandy floor of a vast desert that unfolded before her eyes. Jenny blinked at the bright reflected sunlight of the southwestern morning. She loved mornings like this when the sun was peeking over the horizon, and the dragonflies flitted around her like dancing fairies.

Ah, she thought happily, *there is no darkness here.*

The grandfather looked at her intently.

"No darkness?" he asked. "Jenny, remember there is no light without darkness. What you see here is an illusion of light. It is the other side of the darkness. Just as there is no light without darkness, there is no day without night, no joy without sorrow, no life without death. Each is a part of the other. We are here to learn to respect the importance of balance."

Jenny shook her head.

"I don't understand, Grandfather. Watch the dragonflies. They only come out in the sun. They are happy creatures. They always make me smile, even when I am sad or lonely. They make me feel safe, like everything will be all right. They are creatures of the light, not the darkness."

"Jenny, do you remember the first time you knew the dragonflies made you feel everything would be all right?"

Jenny though carefully. Then she remembered.

"A few years ago my grandma came to live with us. I loved having her there. She baked, she told stories, and she tucked me in at night. I didn't even need a night-light then. I was always safe. She was my best friend. Then one really dark night I heard voices in the hall. I got out of bed and saw some men taking Grandma out in a bed with wheels. She was really sick. Everyone kept telling me Grandma would be home soon, but she never came back."

Jenny's eyes began to sparkle with the tears she tried to hold back. She remembered that dark night so well. She never trusted the darkness after that night.

"For a few weeks after that night I cried all the time. But one day, when I was sitting outside, the dragonflies came into the yard. I had never seen so many! They looked like they were dancing. They just made me smile. I guess that's why I love to see them. They remind me of the first time I smiled after we lost Grandma."

The grandfather smiled as he knelt before her and wiped the tears that were beginning to fall.

"Jenny, it is time for you to stop fearing the darkness. It was not the darkness that took your grandma. It was the Creator choosing the time for her to return to her true home. But he let her send you a message. She told you she was safe and happy."

"She did?"

CHAPTER 17

Jenny: The Messengers

"It is time for your final lesson. It is time for you to see through the darkness of the night that has caused your fear. You blame the darkness that is nothing more than the other half of the light. Now you will come to understand death is just the other side of life. And just as the dark and light have no end, life and death have no end.

Long ago, in the times of the old ones, a great evil came to the earth, intent on destroying the children placed here by the Creator.

The evil wandered the earth, destroying the young and old alike. The people were afraid and traveled many days to seek the wise advice of the great elder medicine man of the desert.

He listened to the people, heard their fears, and thought long and hard through many dark nights. Then he called them to his fireside.

'You must send the young people to battle the enemy. This enemy is strong, and your children will often feel powerless to defeat him. Some may be lost but the battle will be won by their strong hearts.'

The people were afraid to send their children, but the wise chief told them, 'It is the responsibility of our family to protect our people. Keep your children safe at home. I will send my own sons to search for and kill this evil lurking in the shadows.'

The chief's sons searched the earth for many years. They traveled to lands they had heard of only in stories and saw things they had never imagined. They heard the stories of the evil, but were not able to find where it hid.

One night, when the stars were dimmed by high gray clouds and the moon slept behind the shadow of the earth, the evil struck. It attacked the brave sons of the mighty chief. They fought with courage and in the end defeated the evil that had been destroying their loved ones. As they rejoiced, they realized their youngest brother was missing. They searched and searched.

'He is gone,' said the eldest with sorrow. 'The evil must have consumed him.'

The brothers returned to their home and told the chief of all that had occurred. A great sadness came over the village at the loss of the young brother.

The chief returned alone to the great medicine man of the desert.

'I gave you my son to fight this evil, to make this world a better place, and you allowed him to be destroyed by the evil. Now he is lost to all of us forever.'

The medicine man sat in silence and then looked up into the grief-filled eyes of the father standing before him.

'Sit,' he commanded in a soft yet firm voice.

'First, you must know this. The evil that attacked your son did not destroy him. The Creator often reaches out and touches those who need his protection in ways we cannot understand. Your son is protected for eternity. I have seen the other side of this universe. I have heard the voices there, and I will tell you this: there is joy and peace there. Our children, our elders, all who walk in that world have that same protection. Your sorrow is not for your son who has crossed, but for those he left behind. Remember, our Creator is a parent too. And he mourns for his lost children. Knowing this sadness himself, he gives us a gift of comfort.'

'When your loved one crosses into the next world, one of the first sights to greet him will be the messengers. They are there to surround each soul as it begins its new journey. These tiny messengers are a gift from the Creator to the soul moving on and to those who remain behind.

There is only one creature with this ability, the ability to move between the worlds. When each soul is at peace, when the soul finds its comfort and home, a message will be sent to those who grieve its loss.

The Creator molded one beautiful and perfect creation for this sacred task. The dragonfly.

Each spirit, as it rests in peace, is surrounded by these tiny creatures. They are the spirit's messengers to this world of men. They flit through the sunlight, reflecting the beautiful colors of the next world. They remind us each time they skim into view that our loved ones are happy and safe. They let us know, while the spirit may have left an emptiness here, it will watch over us with love until it is our time to make that journey.'

The medicine man smiled as he watched the face of the father. It was then he knew.

'They have visited you,' he said with absolute certainty.

The father smiled through his tears. 'They have.'"

Jenny looked at the old man in wonder. "Those dragonflies were messengers?"

"Of course."

CHAPTER 18

The End...and the Beginning

Joe watched as Jenny walked toward him from the far side of the campfire. She looked the same but, in some way, different. He shook his head. *I guess I'm a little different too*, he thought.

Jenny needed to face her fears. She needed to understand her fears are normal, but letting them rule her life is wrong. She looks like she knows something she didn't know before. I like that. My little buddy is on her way!

"Joe, was it real? Did it all really happen? No one will ever believe where I have been and what I did tonight!"

"Jenny, do you believe it?"

"Absolutely!"

"Then that's all that matters. I believe you. I know it happened. I was there, sort of."

"What do you mean, sort of?"

Jenny was confused. She knew he was there. She had seen him every time she came back. He had never broken his promise and left her. Never.

"Well, while you were gone, the wolf and owl came for me too. But they left a part of my spirit for you. I told them I couldn't leave you. They told me I had to learn what should be, not what could be, but what should be.

What should be? I think finally understand. So many people are living in the past or the future. They feel sorry for themselves because things aren't the way they wanted them to be, or they worry tomorrow won't be what they planned. They forget that today is what we have, what we need to celebrate.

If you look backwards, Jenny, you will have so many regrets. You will think of what you could have done, what you wish you had done, or even the things you did do and wish you hadn't. Lots of people worry about the future all the time. They are afraid they won't have enough money, they are afraid they won't have the job they want, and they are afraid of things that may never even happen. What we should do—did you hear that word, Jenny? *Should.* What we should do is take each day and be the best we can be for this day. We should always remember who we are and the people over the generations who made us into the people we have become. We should take the best of ourselves and use that to be kind, to understand, to learn, to work hard, to help someone else, to laugh, and to love the people in our lives.

Take today to be the person you want to be. Never pass up a chance to be the person you always wished you could be, and you will be that person. If you decide to wait until tomorrow to be that person, you may never get the chance. That's what should be. Each of us should be all that the Creator planned for us to be today. Not tomorrow, not next year. Today."

"I love you, Joe. You're the best friend I ever had."

"Ditto."

As Joe watched Jenny run back to her parents' booth, his eyes shone with pleasure. She would tell them all she had learned this night, and knowing them, they would believe the incredible story of her journey to understanding. He smiled, knowing she would be fine.

The drums were starting again, and Joe turned to look across the arena. The dancers were beginning to fill the circle, bringing it to life with color and sound. It was a good night. Then he saw her, the young woman standing near the drummers. She was about his age, pretty, dressed in jeans and a fringed jacket. *Navajo*, he thought. She looked up, caught his eye and smiled. And suddenly he knew—the circle could begin again....

EPILOGUE

The night air was warm and calm as Owl flew down from the ebony sky to land on Wolf's broad back. They had come to the end of another journey and they needed these last moments together.

"Well?" There was concern in Wolf's voice.

Owl was thinking of all that had occurred during this long night of travel.

"We have more lessons to share with Joe. He is still young and he will continue to ask questions. Perhaps we will get to share those lessons with him as he grows older and begins to search for more answers."

Wolf nodded. "And Jenny?"

Owl smiled. "All is well. Her nightlight is finally off."

PART 3

Brodgar

PROLOGUE

As the moon rose high in the summer sky, a dark shape glided across the waters sparkling below. Owl let out a long, low hoot as her eyes scanned the shadows of the rocky coastline.

He can't be here, she thought, *not in this strange and wild land.*

Yet she felt him, just as she had so many times before. She had been drawn to this faraway place by voices she had never before heard. They called to her, reminding her she had a duty, a task to perform.

Where was Wolf? He had to be there, in the darkness, in those shadows. Surely, he had heard the call. Neither of them would ever ignore those voices. They spoke of the lessons ready to be learned.

The darkest of the shadows seemed to move, and suddenly, he was there. Wolf. Her heart was happy; her oldest friend was once more by her side.

"We have come far this night, old friend. Do you know why the voices brought us here?" Owl asked.

Wolf answered thoughtfully, "Our boy has grown to manhood. Our child who walks in two worlds now has two small children of his own. He and his brothers must learn the difficult task of teaching their own young ones to walk the balance between their two lands. They cannot teach their children the lessons of two worlds unless they learn to walk that path as well. The old ones from this land are the voices we heard calling us this night.

It is time for our young men to cross the great water to see how the bridge between these worlds was built."

"How many do we have this time?" Owl asked.

"There are three, more than we have ever had before. They are young still, but they are already wise. They are waiting for us. It is time."

CHAPTER 1

The Ness

There was no summer warmth in this new place, only mist and gentle rain falling softly on the gray stones standing in the fields, like giants frozen in time. Their silhouettes, gathered in circles, appeared to be creatures of fantasy suddenly caught in a wild dance.

In the distance, the silence was broken by the whining of a bus engine. Then laughter, voices, sounds of the beginning of a new work day echoed across the fields. The sounds startled the lazy sheep who wandered among the stones, looking for the greenest shoots of grass for their breakfast.

Jumping from the bus, Joe and his brothers looked around, seeing the buildings of the ancient ruins for the first time. It had been a long trip from their home in the Arizona desert to the ruins of the Ness of Brodgar, far to the north in Orkney.

"Wow," Scott remarked, "this is awesome. I expected it to look different than the native ruins in Arizona, but it doesn't really."

"Mom said that we needed to talk to the guy in charge before we could grab trowels and head into the pits! Check out all those rocks and mud. I can't wait to start digging!"

"What was his name again?" asked Josh.

"Nick something."

"Let's jump down and take a look in the pit while we wait," Joe was anxious to get started.

"I think you are going to need to wait on that!" cautioned a man with gray whiskers and an Indiana Jones hat. "No one just 'jumps' into these ruins without a lot of instruction. Step on the wrong rock or the wrong piece of dirt, and you have just wiped out thousands of years of knowledge. There's a lot of history down there. Oh, by the way, that 'guy' your mother wanted you to find, Nick? You just found him. Your introduction to the Ness is about to begin."

CHAPTER 2

Lessons from the Past

The hut was small yet brightly lit. Chairs, buckets, plastic trays, and brushes covered the tabletops. Boxes with strange numbers and letters were stacked from floor to ceiling against every wall. A small window let in the filtered light shining down on the paper-lined tabletop. Rocks and dirt seemed to be everywhere. What was this stuff? They had hoped to find ancient treasures, signs of a great civilization that dated back to before recorded time. Instead, there were dusty, dirt-covered bags, and all with these numbers, meaning…what?

The woman in charge of this small, cluttered space seemed to be expecting them. She sat quietly at the table, working her way through the bags, writing down details as she went. She seemed pleased as she carefully looked at it all. Hearing the door open, she looked up and smiled.

"Your mother said she was going to send her sons to us." The woman grinned. "And she said you would look at this room with those exact expressions on your faces! That's okay. She had the same look her first day here as well. She learned quickly, and so will you."

Introducing herself, Anne spoke of the wonders that laid beneath Brodgar's dirt if only you learned to look through the eyes of an explorer.

"It may look like dirt now, but you will quickly learn to recognize each piece of stone, bone, and flint. You will begin to see the folk who lived here long ago as people, much like we are today, just without the modern tools that make our lives easier and a lot less interesting."

Anne reached into a tray and brought out a tiny rock.

"What do you think this is?" she asked.

She handed the rock to Josh, who, turning it over in his hand, started to smile. The stone was less than an inch long, toffee-colored, smooth, shaped with a straight edge with tiny notches in it.

"It's a piece of a flint knife, a scrap broken from a beautiful whole," Anne said.

Josh smiled at her; this tiny piece of flint was the beginning of the journey. He was anxious to get started.

CHAPTER 3

Science and Magic

"Your mother came here understanding her native traditions. She was looking for a connection to her blood that was born here, far from everything she grew up knowing. She is quite the storyteller. She believes there is a story for every occasion, and she is right. There is.

She believes we find history in stories, in oral tradition, legends handed down through time. She can tell a long history of your family based entirely on what she has learned from listening. Here she learned to see that history in the archaeology, through the eyes of science and research. It took a while to get her to understand there is a way for science and tradition to live in harmony in your heart.

And of course, there is always time to share your favorite story. The legends of the past can help everyone, even archaeologists, bring yesterday to life. When you look into the structures at the Ness, what do you see?"

"Dirt, wooden planks, tarps, tools." Joe was first to answer. "And probably some things you can't see."

He knew there was more here than met the eye. He was giving the answer he thought she wanted, and he watched her carefully, hoping for a positive response.

Anne smiled, nodding her head. "I see the people who came here five thousand years ago. I know they had to travel to get to this place. I try to imagine what they did once they arrived. They came to gather together. They didn't live here. Did they come to trade, to worship their gods, to meet their friends and families, to arrange marriages? They exchanged ideas, had great feasts, and celebrated the events of nature watching the movement of the sky, the sun and the moon, and the great constellations.

Their children played here, and they told their stories here. The bones, stones, and flint we bring into this little hut are ancient, five thousand years old. These are the tools, the equipment, and the rubbish left by clever people who built walls, dwellings, and great halls, who decorated and painted the walls, who made beautiful things. These rocks were carefully made into tools, utensils, and things lovely to look at and hold. The flint was worked for scraping and drilling, to make weapons too. These were people far more sophisticated than you might imagine. They were farmers who worked the land, understanding it and the surrounding sea and lochs well. They raised herds of cattle and flocks of sheep. They were not people who sat around small fires, living in caves and eating raw meat.

But there is a balance in these buildings, and that balance is why your mother sent you here. During her time here, she told us she could feel the spirits of what she called "the old ones." She told us they seemed to be at peace, pleased that we had come.

She watched as diggers from all backgrounds and round the world became detectives, investigating the buildings for clues to all that may have occurred here. She saw them leave, taking what they had learned from this place to share with archaeologists, anthropologists, botanists, and biologists. She saw the value of the science, the importance of the discoveries.

But she fell in love with the magic, mystery, and spirit of the Ness. She insisted the sense of this place, its magic, needed to be preserved along with the science. Many of us, the archaeologists who have worked with the Ness, understand her passion well. We need to balance the science and the magic, like her. We hope visitors understand the connection. Maybe they miss it when they first come but get its specialness by the time they leave. Your mother felt it. She saw it instantly.

This is to explain why she wanted you to come here. Scientists can dig and discover, but the lives of the ancient people of this land will only live on if we all speak of what we have learned here, if their stories continue to be told. Now we want you too, to be a part of that chorus of voices. You came here to learn, and now you will leave to tell the stories of the Ness of Brodgar, of the past as we understand it more and more, of the place of gathering it has become again, and of the people of this ancient island where 'the old ones' are always in our minds."

CHAPTER 4

The Call of the Standing Stones

It had been over a week. They were dirty, sore, and tired. Yet there was an excitement to this work. Every day, sometimes every hour, a treasure was pulled from the dirt and mud. Students and seasoned archaeologists would find glimmers of a past civilization that they carefully removed from the ruins, preserving exactly when and where the discovery was made.

Each day began with anticipation. Throughout the day diggers grinning with discovery would arrive at the door of the little hut with objects untouched by human hands for thousands of years. Each tray was a mystery of its own. What were the stories behind the beautiful, colorfully grained stone axe heads, the pieces of delicately grooved pottery, or the incised stone slabs? What did they do with that pottery ball? Did they really paint walls thousands of years ago? Why? They asked many questions, enthralled by each detailed explanation they received.

Tray upon tray of rocks, tools, flint, and bone were dried, cleaned, tagged, and bagged to be studied when summer had ended, and the long, dark winter of the far north descended on the little island.

They had been waiting for the weekend. There was no digging, no cleaning or inventory to complete. It was time for a day of wandering at the Ness, exploring the surroundings and learning about the long-ago time in this ancient land.

As their bus arrived at the site, they were disappointed to see the mist rolling in across the water and fields stretching lazily out from the Ness at the center. Their companions headed to the buildings that provided shelter from the cold and damp, knowing the rain would soon begin to fall.

"I need to see the standing stones." Scott had always been fascinated by ancient structures. "I want to get closer to them."

CHAPTER 5

Dingishowie

"Take care," Anne warned.

She had overheard Scott's excitement about exploring the stones standing like sentinels at either end of the thin strip of land cutting through the dark water.

"You have no idea what strange things occur in our ancient places here on Orkney. I will worry about 'when' you might be." She smiled.

"You mean 'where' we might be, don't you?" Josh looked confused.

"No, Josh. I'll worry about 'when' you might be. Let me explain.

A fine fiddle player, the best fiddle player in Orkney, Tam Bichan, came home one night, past the ancient mound, or howe of Dingishowie, thinking he could hear music on the air. As he passed Dingishowie, he met a peedie man [a small man] who clearly knew who Tam was and his reputation as a musician. He stopped Tam and invited him to come and join him and his friends, to play and dance the night away. Tam's pleasure in his music was great, and he accepted the invitation, following the peedie man into the mound, through a door Tam had never seen before.

They played and drank and danced and sang the night long, and Tam felt he'd never played so well, nor had such a memorable night of music making.

The next morning Tam woke, picked up his fiddle, and headed for the howie door, into a beautiful morning. He walked the well-worn and familiar road home, his head in the clouds, humming the new tunes he'd learned, up the loan to his house, in through the door, and there by the fireside sat a man he'd never seen before. Tam looked about himself in puzzlement—some things he recognized, others were unknown to him. The man at the fire gazed at him, shocked.

"'Tam Bichan, is that you?'

Tam nodded and asked, 'And who are you?'

The man by the fire asked, 'Where have you been? We thought we'd lost you years ago.'

Tam Bichen had spent the night with the trows, the magic folk who dwell in Orkney's howes and knowes—the folk who capture the minds of human folk and keep them entranced in the trows' world for years and years and years, finally releasing the human folk [or maybe just some of them?] back into the human world, where the holes of the missing years have somehow to be understood and explained.

"So be careful as you pass those ancient places built thousands of years ago, now grass-covered mounds in Orkney's landscape. Don't be beguiled by music and hospitable, peedie strangers.

"Now off you go. Have your adventure exploring the standing stones. We will watch for you coming back—soon."

CHAPTER 6

The Guides

A heavy mist rolled across the damp field, making the stones nearly invisible. They walked slowly toward them, taking care with each step not to stumble on the uneven ground. The stones appeared to grow before them, getting taller and darker against the gray fog.

"What is that?" Josh's voice broke through the mist. "Over there."

The figure was large, hulking, moving slowly in the mist from behind the largest of the stones. As it approached, it began to take shape and became Wolf. Joe smiled.

"Here? Now? Really?"

Wolf walked softly across the wet grass, stopping by Joe's side. He allowed Joe to reach down and pat his neck softly. They were old friends; they had journeyed together before.

Joe looked up into the sky, knowing he would be able to see little of what might be above him. Still, he knew that where Wolf was, Owl would be found as well.

She flew quietly down from her perch on the highest stone, settling softly on Wolf's strong back. Looking from one brother to the next, she smiled to herself. This was going to be different than before. She had a surprise in store for the travelers, something that would change their view of the world forever.

"There are more lessons to be learned, more adventures to unfold, more people to meet. Are you ready for our journey?"

All three looked at one another, nodded, and turned back to Owl.

"We're ready."

"We will have another with us this time. In this new land, we must be respectful and request one of the ancestors of this world to join us just as we would expect a traveler to our land to ask us to guide them.

Joe, do you remember Sarah? She brought you here once before, teaching you to understand you are of two great people from either side of the waters. She taught you to embrace all those who helped to make you the very special person you are."

He remembered her well. She had brought him to an understanding of the two paths his family had walked in their past. He had learned well from her, sharing her message with his brothers who stood with him beneath the great standing stones.

"You told me you would return, Joe. I see you have brought your brothers. I am pleased, as they too need to learn all the past has to teach us. Now, my friends, I will ask you the question we will be trying to answer through our newest journey.

Are we different? I do not mean each of us, for each of us is unique in our own very special way. I want us to learn if people can come from different worlds yet be the same in their hearts? Can our histories walk in different lands yet meet as one in our spirit?

Your grandmother was Native American. Her spirit was born of her history and culture across the sea. Your grandfather was from this land, learning from our ancient ways. How could they come together to create a world where you were a possibility?

This is the question we seek to answer. Are you ready?"

CHAPTER 7

The Dance of the Giants

The standing stones towered around them, casting ghostly shadows through the swirling mists. Sarah reached down, stroking Wolf's thick fur as she thought carefully. It was time to begin, but she must take care with such an important task.

"This is where we will start, in this place. Look around you. Do you see the others?"

The three young men looked around, confused by the question. There were no others, only the three of them and their guides. They turned slowly in the mists, straining to see past the stones that surrounded them.

"Ah, you don't understand. But you will soon enough. There are many of the old ones, the first people of this ancient land who will appear strange to you. Think about what Anne told you, her story of the trows. She has already taught you there are different beings here. That was your first important lesson. They will help you learn that listening is not done only with your ears. You must listen to the voices connecting yesterday, today, and tomorrow with your hearts and the blood that binds you to this land. Close your eyes, and their voices will speak to you.

The old ones of this island came here from far to the north, across the icy sea. Some of them were great giants, fierce and angry, proud and fearless. They loved to compete with one another, often fighting and tossing giant boulders across the fields to see who was the mightiest. Some could throw a stone for miles, leaving mysterious, lone, standing stones scattered across their new homeland.

But in certain places across our land, you will find these quiet circles, standing in green fields, unending rings of wonder. I told you to listen, standing in the mists that have been a part of this island for eternity. Do you hear the voices?

Once, in the long-ago yesterdays of time, these giants roamed our land. They were fair-skinned, with long red hair. They were proud, strong, and tall, fearing no living creature. They ruled their spot on this earth. The only thing in heaven or on earth able to harm these creatures was the golden light of the sun's rays. One night, when the moon was full and the stars dotted the heavens, a group of giants came here, to the Ness, where you have been spending your days searching for the past.

"'It was a bonny evening, and the giants were in quite a festive mood. Now, these giants loved to sing and dance, and when the music would begin, they would all join in the festivities. The group had been traveling for many nights with no time for leisure or fun. When one of the giants pulled out his grand fiddle and began to play, they were delighted by the rousing tune and began to dance.

They danced and sang throughout the night. They shared great barrels of mead, told exciting tales of adventures of old, and laughed together as only old friends can do. They never noticed the sky getting lighter and lighter. Suddenly the first blessed ray of the morning sun crept over the horizon. In horror they watched as the sun rose, lighting the fields around them with its golden hue. The dancing slowed as the fiddler drew his bow with more and more difficulty. In their joy, they had forgotten their only foe, the powerful sun that now shone upon them, turning them forever into the circle of standing stones before you."

They looked up, seeing the giants captured forever in their stillness. They suddenly remembered their first impression of the stones, the fanciful vision of a wild dance. Had giants truly been here, in these fields, feeling the joy and wonder of the music and the beauty of the night?

CHAPTER 8

The Protectors

Owl had been sitting quietly on Wolf's shoulder as Sarah told the story of the stone circle, weaving the magic of the summer night with the dancing giants of long, long ago. She closed her big, dark eyes, remembering something from deep in her own past.

"Wolf," she spoke softly. "Do you remember our stone giants?"

He nodded his head. He too was thinking back to the story they had been told many years ago of the magical beings who protected the mountains and valleys of the native people far to the north in their own land.

"The winter wind lives far to the north in our land. It is the land of the salmon, the grizzly bear, the buffalo, and the mountain sheep. Summer is short, and the people work hard to ensure there is food for the cold nights when the winter wind comes to claim his territory. There is plenty in this place, berries growing wild by the river, pumpkin, corn, sunflowers, and squash.

It was a safe place where all could live in harmony with Mother Earth. But the beauty of the land beckoned the new strangers who had come from across the sea to explore and conquer what, to them, was a new world.

But those who lived there knew it was a truly ancient world. It remains a world where everything has purpose and meaning. To the people of our land, even the rocks others see as insignificant beneath their feet have spirits and memories.

If you go to places in our land where the rocks are called 'the grandfathers,' you may see the giant stone towers we call the hoodoos. The visitors marvel at the intricate balanced rocks, stretching tall toward the beautiful blue skies. They stare and wonder at how they might have been formed. We who have walked these lands for generations know how they were formed and why they stand as silent sentinels as the sun shines down on them.

When the intruders came so long ago, many did not respect our people, our lands, or our way of life. They wanted only to change what had been since the beginning of time. Our people were driven from their traditional lands, the forests were destroyed for the timber, and the game was hunted to near extinction.

What they did not know was this land to the north was also home to the sleeping giants. As the sun slipped below the edge of the earth each evening, they would awaken from their deep slumber and wander the countryside. They were peaceful and bothered no one. They loved their homeland just as the native people loved it.

When morning came, just as with the giants of the stone circles in this land, the giants would turn to stone. They would be frozen by the bright light of day into the towering hoodoos of granite that baffled unknowing visitors.

Even the gentlest of the Creator's beings can be moved to fear or anger when threatened, and as legend tells us, this is what happened to the stone giants of this beautiful place. Each night, as they woke from their slumber, they were faced with more intruders, more destruction, and more sorrow from the first people of the land. The giants, wanting to do whatever they could to help their neighbors, would stand on the hillsides, tossing great boulders into the paths where the intruders might pass. They would search for those places where the new people were resting before pushing on at daybreak to take more of a land that belonged to others. In the morning the newcomers would awaken to rock slides and slate walls barring their progress.

Sadly, the hoodoos could only slow the inevitable. The intruders would not be stopped, and the native people of our land lost everything as the unwelcome visitors advanced across our vast and ancient home.

The giants in both lands were large and powerful. They were feared by humankind, and they truly were masters of their worlds. Yet, as you see, they were both at the mercy of something as simple, yet as powerful, as the rays of the morning sun."

CHAPTER 9

The Spiderweb

"One need not be a giant to make an enormous difference in the world. Have you ever felt small and unimportant? As the world has changed, we animals have come to understand wisdom and strength can hide in the smallest of creatures. But you must understand, we animals remember far more than you humans have forgotten," Owl stated simply.

She sat quietly, thinking, wanting to be certain her words would be understood.

"Do you believe size and strength are all that is needed to protect and guide the people? Yes, giants walked the worlds of both of your ancestors, here on this island and far across the sea on the land we call Turtle Island. This first stop on our travels has shown us one small vision of the long-ago footsteps that traveled the same roads in time.

It is important to remember one need not be a giant to have the strength and courage to make changes in this world. Even the smallest of creatures has great power. In the long-ago time, people searched for symbols to guide them to do great things. They needed to compare themselves and their quests to the wisdom and wonder of the natural world.

One morning the chief of a small tribe of native people was hunting. His people were hungry, and it was his job as leader to provide for them. As he searched for game in the shadows of the deep forest, he had time to think and wonder about how to share his visions with the people of his community.

'I must give them an animal symbol, one that will make them work toward being strong, courageous, and careful. When they see this symbol, they will want to model their behavior after its power.'

Then, in a sunlit clearing, the chief saw the footprints. They were the prints of a very large deer. The footprints alone were enough to convince the chief this animal would provide food for many weeks. He stepped back into the shadows, treading lightly on the pine needles that carpeted the forest floor. He would track the great deer and it would be his.

The deer! he thought suddenly. *What a perfect symbol for our people. The buck deer is brave, swift, and careful. He provides for his family and watches for danger. His antlers grow taller each year, and he looks like the king of the forest as he stands on the hilltops. Yes, the deer will be our guide.*

The chief saw the prints were fresh and knew he was getting closer to his prey. He began to run, faster and faster through the brush of the forest. The tracks told him he was almost there. He became breathless with the effort of running and the excitement of the chase.

'Ahh!' he cried out. 'What is that?'

He had run headfirst into the largest, strongest spiderweb he had ever seen. The chief fell down onto the path and looked up in anger. The web had been spun between two trees, across the very trail he needed to follow. As he jumped up, he searched the web, looking for the offending insect that had blocked his hunt.

There was the spider, sitting in the corner of her web. The chief, frustrated and irritated, swung out at the spider, but she jumped out of his reach, looked at him in confusion, and spoke.

'My friend, why are you running through the forest, looking only at the ground? If you looked up, you would see the dangers and obstacles before you.'

The chief, realizing his anger at the spider was pointless, replied, 'I am hunting a great deer. He will be food for my people as winter approaches. But even more important, I am searching for a symbol of strength and courage for my people.'

The spider looked thoughtfully at the great chief. She shook her head and smiled at him.

'Ah, I see you do not understand. I am that symbol, my friend.'

The chief laughed out loud. 'You? You are so insignificant I did not even notice you as I tracked the great deer. You cannot be a symbol to inspire my people.'

'My friend, look at me carefully. See me as I truly am, and you will understand my strength. I have great patience. I do not move swiftly or carelessly. I take my time. I watch and wait. I am willing to try and try again until I succeed. I work tirelessly, knowing all things will come to me. These are the things your people must learn if they are to be strong and successful. And I stopped you, a great chief, didn't I?' she said, smiling.

The chief looked at the tiny spider. He saw the intricate web that was strong, useful, and powerful. Then as the shadows of the forest began to lengthen into dusk, he nodded. He understood at last. His people could learn much from the spider. They would learn power comes from far greater gifts than size and strength.

And that is how the small, insignificant spider became a symbol of power and perseverance to the people of the tribe."

CHAPTER 10

Determination

Sarah looked thoughtful. She was remembering another story of a long-ago time, much like Owl's tale of the tiny spider.

"Scotland, too, learned much from the lowly spider. It is truly a mystery how thousands of miles and centuries of time lay between these two stories while the message is very much the same.

Robert the Bruce, one of Scotland's bravest and best-loved heroes lived long, long ago. He fought to give his people the freedom they wanted so badly. Just as your people across the sea fought to be themselves, the Scots did as well.

He had fought many battles. He was both brave and wise, but he lived in dangerous times. A great army was sent to defeat Robert and the Scottish people. His army was getting smaller as it lost battle after battle. Finally, it seemed there was no hope in sight, and poor Robert became sad and discouraged.

Legend tells us, he sought shelter in the darkness of a remote cave where he lay alone for many days. He knew the entire country and all its people were counting on him, and he had failed them over and over. He tried once, twice, three times, and more. Each time, he failed. In each battle, he was defeated. He was sad, tired, and in pain. His soldiers had fought and died for freedom, yet he could not force himself to fight one more time. He could not bear to see any more of his friends lost in battle. Here he was now, in this cave, sad and alone. He knew all he had worked for, fought for, was out there, and he could do nothing.

Then one morning, as the dawn broke, he lay in the damp cave as the rain approached, falling softly on the fields before him. Not wanting to brave the cold and wet, he lay back on the floor of the cave.

There, in the corner by the entrance to the cave, he noticed a wee brown spider. She gazed through the darkness, straining to see what wonders awaited in the shadows lurking all about. She seemed to be listening to the darkness, to music Robert could not hear. Bored, he watched with disinterest as she began to spin her web. She spun one long, sparkling strand, and then she was ready.

As he watched, the inquisitive, little creature tried to throw the end of her web to the other side of the entry door. She knew this cave was so much more than a dark and dismal hole in the side of the great mountain. She could feel there was something waiting for her there in the darkness. The cave and its shadows told her of adventure, discovery, perhaps magic awaiting her. If she could just reach the other side, oh, what wonders she would find! She swung her web strand higher and higher. But she failed, falling short.

He watched as she tried again and again to reach the other side. Once she almost made it but missed, swinging wildly at the end of the single strand of web. Fascinated now by her determination, Robert sat up. He held his breath as she tried again. Six times she would begin to swing higher and higher. Six times she fell short.

Poor little beastie, I understand, he thought. *I know what it is like to try so hard and fail again and again. It's hopeless.*

But then, with her next attempt, she reached out, and straining with all her strength, she stretched out her tiny legs, and success! She reached the other side. Six times she tried and failed, but on her last attempt, she made it! She had succeeded when failure seemed her only option.

What an amazing creature was this tiny spider! Robert lay back, closing his eyes, remembering. He saw himself as a small child, first learning to walk, to climb stairs, to explore his world. His nursemaids would pick him up over and over as he worked toward his goal of independence. He could hear their words, 'Never give up! Keep trying, my boy.'

They had loved telling him each step he took was taking him toward his goal of greatness. He had laughed as they stood him up on his sturdy, little legs over and over.

'You will be a leader, a great man. But you must first learn that each step leads to the next. Soon you will run, young Robert!'

"Robert the Bruce was reminded by this tiny yet very determined spider the only sure way to fail was to stop trying. He went from that cave back to his people, urging them to have the courage and strength he had observed in one of the smallest of creatures. Just as with the chief in Owl's story, Robert found strength and courage come from spirit, not from size."

CHAPTER 11

Beneath the Mound

"It's time to travel on a bit," Sarah told them. "We have things to see and lessons to learn."

She began to walk away from the stone circle, the churning dark waters and the Ness.

"We need to go that way," Scott was heading toward a gentle mound rising from the mist-covered moor. "I want to see what's over there."

Sarah hesitated. "Perhaps we should study that interesting little spot from a distance. Here on the island we are very respectful of our mounds and ancient places. You never know what might be hidden just beneath the surface.

Here we have magical creatures, fairies, witches, and the giants and trows with whom you have already become acquainted. Most people never see these creatures who live among them while maintaining their distance. But still you must take great care when these beings are near. They are tricksters, and they can lure humans into very uncomfortable situations.

Let me tell you of one such creature. He is called the Hogboon. Hogboons are solitary creatures, living in old burial mounds such as the one we are approaching. These rather-unpleasant beings are rarely seen, although those who have happened across them say they appear much like tiny, old men with beards, huge, pointed ears, and bulging eyes.

Should a Hogboon decide to live in a mound on your land, you must know how to care for him, or he will cause you nothing but problems. He always expects to eat well, and it is your job to be certain he gets all he desires, fresh bread, milk, vegetables, and cheese. Never walk on his mound, for he believes it to be his, not yours. He will remain happy, and your life will be uneventful as long as you treat him with great kindness and respect.

Now, many years ago a Hogboon happened to make his home in a mound on the farm of an industrious, young man. The two lived together in peace and prosperity for many years. The young farmer cared for the Hogboon, making certain no one disturbed his home and seeing that he was well fed at all times. He never failed to bring him his share of the goods produced by the farm and often poured a bit of ale on the mound as a treat.

The farmer became prosperous, but he was sad and lonely. It was time to find a wife and build a family to keep him company and help run the farm. Off the farmer went to town, looking for the perfect wife to share his life. Soon he found her, and, delighted, he brought her home to begin their life together.

The farmer's wife was a bright and cheerful girl, but she was from the town and knew little of life in the country. Still, anxious to be a good partner to her new husband, she learned quickly. She cooked and cleaned and tended the garden by the house. She sewed clothing for herself and her husband and minded the money carefully so they would be able to save for the things that would make their life better…

But, sadly, she knew nothing of Hogboons. She never left milk out for him or baked extra bread. She dried the extra vegetables and stored them for winter, never giving the Hogboon his share. The Hogboon waited and waited, but she never learned the importance of treating him as a respected member of the farm family.

After some time he came to resent her neglect. He was angry with the farmer who had, it seemed, forgotten his presence entirely. It was time to remind them how important it was to keep him happy.

Soon the farm began to fall into disrepair. Walls would crumble overnight, leaks would appear in the roof, animals were falling ill, vegetables were dying on the vine. The wife found her bread burning in the oven. The cows and goats gave little milk, and it quickly soured. The once-prosperous farm was dying, and they had no idea what to do.

One morning the farmer awakened before the sun was up. Looking out his window at the sun slowly trying to peek over the horizon, he suddenly realized what was behind all the troubles. The Hogboon was quite angry and was letting them know his true feelings.

The couple had nothing left to offer him. They barely had enough food for themselves, and what they had would never make the Hogboon happy. The farmer realized there was only one thing to do. They would move to the other end of the island, far from the angry Hogboon in the mound. They would start a new life, away from the neglected creature dwelling on their land.

Soon they had permission to set up their home on another part of the island, leaving the disgruntled Hogboon behind. With great excitement, they packed their few belongings and set out across the hills to their new home. In his arms the farmer carried a small, carved chest holding the few treasures he and his wife had kept in their little home. Their one pony carried the churn so they would have fresh butter in their new home once the cows and goats began producing good milk again. They sang as they walked, ready to begin their lives over far from the troubles of the past few years. Once again, life would be good, joyful, and prosperous.

As they arrived at the new farmhouse, overlooking the sea and rocks below, they were startled by a rattling sound. They looked around, bewildered.

Suddenly the lid of the carved chest the farmer carried flew off, turning over and over in the early evening air as the Hogboon jumped out, crying, 'Just look at our wonderful new home! Thank you for bringing me along with your other family treasures!' And he laughed and laughed as he ran off to find the new spot he would call his own.

It is always good to remember we cannot run away from our troubles. They travel with us until we must finally deal with them.

We take both our fortune and our misfortune when we move from place to place in this world. Take care with how you treat both the mortal beings you see each day and the magical folk you may never see. They are always a part of our lives."

Wolf had listened carefully to Sarah as she spoke of the Hogboon and the respect that one must have for the magical creatures and the spirits of this island.

"We, too, have respect for our spirits and magical beings, creatures who walk in other worlds different from those of the living. Many of our native people believe the spirits walk among us at all times. Great care is taken not to offend these spirits. We do not mention their names, or they could come to torment us. We never leave windows broken, or the spirits could come into our homes to cause trouble. And never call a whirlwind a name. It could be a spirit waiting for you to call it to you. Our elders still tell the stories of witches, monsters, mermaids, and giant animals, just as yours tell of the Hogboon. It would seem that we share this heritage of many worlds in our two lands. Our stories may be different, but I see that they come from that same space between this world and the next."

CHAPTER 12

Stolen Stories

Scott smiled at Sarah. "You know, it's lucky we're here and not at home right now."

"Why is that?" she asked, looking curious.

"In some parts of Indian Country, no one can tell stories in the summertime. It is a taboo, forbidden. There is a good reason stories are told that way in our country.

Our elders would tell the stories in the wintertime. When it was really cold and the snow came. The people would stay in their lodges or gather around campfires. They pulled their blankets around themselves and sat together in the darkness. That is when the grandmothers and grandfathers would begin to tell the old tales. They would take the time to teach the history and culture to the next generation. They would tell the little ones how the world began, how our people came to walk the earth, and why the animals live as they do.

Long ago they would tell the stories all the time, but then something strange happened, and it changed everything."

Sarah sat down on a large rock, readying herself to hear a story sure to be exciting. She found the tales of this far-off land to be almost magical. She knew these young men were sharing their own world with her, and she was anxious to hear what came next.

"What was this thing that changed storytelling forever?"

"I hope I can tell it to you the way our mother told the story to us. One day, in the early summer of a year in the old time, a mother and her youngest children left their village for a short walk down to the stream to get water. It was a perfect morning: birds singing, clear water running over the rocks, and wildflowers everywhere. Before heading back, they sat down by the side of the stream bed, and the mother began to tell a story to the children. I heard it was an exciting story, but no one knows for sure."

"Why does no one know? I am thinking such a great tale would be easy to remember."

"Well, it's strange you say that. You see, the story was so exciting when they all returned to their village, the children ran to find their friends to tell them the story. But when they opened their mouths to repeat the story, they couldn't recall a single word. Not one.

Angry with themselves, they ran home. Bursting inside, they raced to their mother, crying out, 'We can't remember the story from this morning. Can you tell us again?'

'Of course,' she replied simply. She sat down and began her story. But as she opened her mouth, nothing came out. Nothing, not one word of the story remained. 'I don't remember.' She was puzzled. 'I have known that story all my life, but it's gone, simply gone.'

Strange as this had been, they all went about their day and evening. By morning they had forgotten about the lost story. There were chores to do and games to play. Summer was a busy time.

That afternoon the mother gathered her youngest children together, and just as they had done the day before, they walked to the stream to fetch water for the evening. And once again, she settled herself on the bank to tell stories to the little ones.

Heading home, they tried to remember the stories they had just heard. But once again, nothing. The words were gone, as though they had never existed.

For many days words and stories continued to disappear. The people became wary, afraid to speak for fear there would soon be no stories left to tell, and the past would vanish forever.

Then one day, when the breeze was calling, a young woman from the village went down to the stream. She sat under the trees with her tiny, newborn baby and began to tell him a story. She spoke softly, hoping no one would hear. But her older son had followed, creeping along behind the bushes, watching, listening. And then he saw it.

As her words were spoken, wisps of air came from her mouth. They floated gently down on the light summer breeze, falling toward the warm rocks by the streambed.

Sitting silently beneath the trees, sunning herself beside a warm outcropping of rock, sat a small, colorful snake. She had a tiny basket balanced on her head, which she moved carefully as she caught the wisps of words falling from the lips of the young mother.

The boy watched as the story ended, and the young mother filled her water basket and started her walk back to the village. As she walked away, the tiny snake began slithering away. She kept her head very still and straight, not wanting to lose even one of the precious words she had collected. Her own babies would be waiting to hear the wonderful tales she had stolen just for them!

Since that time long ago our people who live where the snakes like to sun themselves in the summer know they must never tell their tales when the snakes are about, eager and ready to steal any story they hear. And that is why their stories are told only when the cold winds begin to blow and the frost greets them at daybreak. That is when the snakes sleep, and the stories come back to life."

CHAPTER 13

The Wee Adder

Sarah listened intently as Scott remembered his mother's words from when he was a child. Snakes stealing stories! Nothing like that could happen here, not in this land where snakes are never seen.

"We tell our stories by the winter fireside as well. When the air turns crisp and the ice begins to form in the corners of the window panes, it becomes the perfect time for a warm cup of tea, a toasty, and a story. Winters here are long and dark. The sun dips low in the afternoon, making the days short and the nights so very long. The dark winter is a good time to tell the old stories of myth and magic. It is as though the spirits of the ancestors feel safe and secure in the short, gray days as the year ends.

But we tell our stories in the springtime as well, when the world comes awake once again. We tell of the giants and fairies who dance and play on warm summer evenings. Spring is when we learn of the old ways: planting, hunting, tracking the stars and planets in the night sky, learning about the valiant deeds of our ancestors.

Summer here is still story time, for we do not need to fear the snakes hiding by the warm rocks, waiting to steal away with our words tucked safely in their baskets.

There may once have been snakes in our land in the long-ago time. But today they have vanished, perhaps by natural causes, perhaps by some ancient magic that drove them far away from our shores. I wonder why they did not choose to live here. No one can know for sure because none of us walks that path where mystery touches realty.

Here on our islands we can share our stories in safety throughout the seasons. A warm summer afternoon is a grand time for sitting in the shadows of the stones and sharing the past.

I can tell you of one wee snake inhabitant who stubbornly stayed below in Scotland when his kind had moved on, looking for a new home. Their little adder is quite small and timid. When people come near, he will quickly leave the place where they have chosen to walk. He has no wish to interact with humanity, never sure what their intentions might be. He would never sit nearby to listen to magical tales of time gone by.

The adder may be small, but if cornered or trapped, his bite can be deadly. Everyone has great respect for his strength and determination to protect himself. They strive to live in peace with him, and as he does with them. This peace is a very good thing.

The important thing to understand is, though we tell our stories at different times, we tell them. Our people, yours and mine together, respect the past by honoring and caring for that past through storytelling. The stories tie our present to our past. When we share them with our children, we share them with the future as well. We want our young ones to learn the old ways, from that time when man could not write his history. Our stories have kept us alive for generation upon generation. Through stories we have learned who we are, we have met our heroes, seen great battles, and we have come to understand we have a history of wonder and value. Each story has a purpose as we weave the fabric of our existence.

The telling of stories is ancient. We both know it must never be lost in time."

CHAPTER 14

Miracles Happen

"Our time together has made me wonder," Sarah said. "You are here, standing right in front of me like three great miracles who might never have come to pass. Somehow, Here met There, and you were able to be born. Have you ever thought of yourselves as improbable beings in this great, wide world?

You are here, walking with me this night for many reasons, and some of those reasons start just to the south of us, in Scotland, far away from your own homeland. You spoke earlier of the invaders, those coming to your lands from other places, seeking to change your world into their world. The Scots, too, faced invaders.

Many centuries ago, Scotland was its own country, filled with proud people who wanted to maintain their way of life. Does that sound familiar to you? It should. The native people of your land were much the same and had similar desires.

For centuries English kings sent their generals to take our land. They came from the south with thousands of soldiers armed and ready to fight for a country belonging to your ancestors. The Scots fought each attack, bravely defending their homeland. Sometimes they won, sometimes they lost. Yet through it all, they held onto their proud belief that this was their land, their country, their culture, and their future.

Finally, on a sad spring day, the Scots met the English army on a windswept, damp, and dreary battlefield called Culloden. The cannons thundered, the claymores glinted in the filtered sunlight, and the battle began. When the day ended, the English army claimed a great victory, and it marked the end of a way of life the Scots had cherished for centuries.

Life became more and more difficult for many of the highland people in Scotland. There was fear and poverty in the land. They could no longer live as their families had lived for centuries."

Sarah smiled at her traveling companions. They looked so sad, but she needed for them to understand without this history they would not exist.

"It's not all bad," she explained. "Many of these Scots boarded ships bound for a better life. They went searching for a place that reminded them of home yet offered peace and the ability to live without fear. Some came to your land. They came as many invaders had come to your home, but they were different.'

The brothers looked at each other, confused by what she was saying. She was telling him that the Scots had come to their homeland, strangers trying to prosper from their resources. Yet she said these invaders were different than the others. They turned their attention back to her as she continued to speak.

"Some of them traveled south, where they found mountains and glens reminding them of their beloved homeland. They found native people living there as they had for centuries. The Scots arrived in peace, honoring the ways of those claiming the land as their ancestral home. They asked permission to stay, offered to help, and agreed to live in peace and harmony with nature.

Others, Scots and Orkadians alike, traveled north, living with the natives of the cold lands of Canada. Even today there can be found descendants of the marriages that took place between the people of Orkney and the mighty native nations of your neighbor to the north.

As time went by, the newcomers became a part of the beautiful lands they had settled in the misty mountains and cold valleys they had grown to love. They found many customs and traditions so similar it was as though they had known one another well in times past. Soon the children began to marry within the clans of the native people and the clans of the newcomers.

That, my dears, is how you came to be born. When the brave son of the local tribe married the lovely, young daughter of a clansman, a miracle began. That miracle stands before me this night."

CHAPTER 15

Mitakuye Oyasin

"Our grandmother was a great storyteller. She handed down our history as her father had told it to her when she was a child," Joe began. "I am not sure how much I remember, but let me try."

"The little boy awakened as the sun began its journey across the desolate plains of his land. He leapt from the warmth of his sleeping area near the fire, excited to start this new adventure. This would be his very first time traveling with the people as they headed farther north than he had ever been.

He had dreamed of this day, his thoughts taking him across the prairies, through the forests, and into the snow-covered mountains far beyond the horizon he knew so well. Each night they would join him in his dreams. The wolf and the owl were always there.

'As you travel,' the wise Owl instructed, 'watch where each step falls. Notice the land, the plants, the animals and the stones. They will teach you, they will guide you, and they will become your family.'

He had not understood, but he was eager to begin this journey to a new place. He had listened to Owl and knew he must do as he had been told. He would watch, listen, and learn.

The ponies were waiting, their breath making clouds of steam in the gray of the breaking day. They were packed with blankets, meat, and hides. The young boy walked at his father's side, his small day pack on his back and his warmest boots tied high on his sturdy little legs.

The days were long, the trail endless. He never complained. This trip was a part of the life of his people. He walked on throughout the daylight, and when the early darkness began to fall, he slept soundly. As the days passed, he forgot what Owl had told him. His mind began to wander as he traveled north. The plants and animals were forgotten as the daydreams took over his tired mind.

Then one night he slept more soundly than before. And he began to dream once again. The wolf and owl were there, as they had been before he started his journey.

"You have forgotten your task." Wolf sounded disappointed. "Owl told you of your relatives along the trail, but you have not watched for them. They are here to teach you."

When he woke the next morning, he remembered. Just as Wolf and Owl always remembered what needed to be done, he now remembered as well.

He saw where the winter animals had wandered aimlessly through the snow, searching for food in the icy forests. He saw the tiny plants, fighting to push their way through the frozen ground, working hard to survive the cold winter. He noticed each rock along the path, unique and strong, providing a solid path for them to walk.

With each passing day he understood more of the world in which he lived. This world was made up of many beings, none more powerful or important than the other. He began to see to see how all beings on this earth were part of the Creator's family. He learned to listen to the four-leggeds, the winged ones, the plants and the rocks, seeing the spirit in each of them.

Still, his most important lesson was still ahead.

At long last, they arrived at the village of their northern relatives. There they found warm lodges, food, and welcome. They also found the others, the strangers from another land with fair skin and light eyes.

These strangers had come from a land far across the great water. They were different than the others who had come before them, taking what they wanted and demanding more. These strangers had asked with respect if they might stay. They learned the language and customs of their new home and family. They had learned the ways of the native people, hunting and fishing, preparing food, tending the fires, and caring for one another.

The boy feared the newcomers, as he had learned to fear those he had seen before. It was time for his final lesson.

Sitting by the fire one cold night when the stars hid behind the clouds, and the moon was a tiny crescent in the sky, he fell into a deep sleep at his father's side. As he slept, he slipped into his dreams, wandering the forests with Wolf and Owl. As Wolf walked silently by his side, Owl flew high into the night sky, looking—as she always did—for any danger lurking nearby. Seeing none, she landed on a low-hanging limb.

'You fear the newcomers.' She was absolute.

'I do.'

'It is wise to fear what you do not know, but never let that fear control you. Never allow it to take away your opportunity to learn and grow. We fear what we do not understand, what is new, or what is unseen.

But in this world, all things, all people, all creatures are related. You must experience the unknown if you are going to learn to understand all your relations. You may not see eye to eye with all of creation, but you must take time to know all you can. Give others of your kind a chance to prove themselves, good or bad. Judge each separately and understand good people come from many places, many cultures, and many lands.

'I will teach you two words, important words. You must always remember them, think about them, repeat them, pray with them, live by them.'

The boy nodded.

'Mitakuye Oyasin,' said Owl, solemnly. 'These two words mean, "We are all related." Remember I said you would meet many from your family along your journey. The animals, the plants, the birds flying high above you, the rocks paving your path—these are all your relations. And the newcomers, the strangers, these people are your relations as well. Remember.'

'I promise. Mitakuye Oyasin.'

Joe looked at his brothers. "Did I forget anything?"

Josh smiled. "Yes, you forgot to tell Sarah that when that little boy grew up and became a father, he watched his eldest son marry one of the strangers."

Sarah looked contently at Josh. "Ah, the journey to the miracle that became you! Two countries, one great ocean, a journey of many miles in a bitter winter. What are the odds that this might happen? You see, a miracle."

CHAPTER 16

Departure

Owl sat on Wolf's broad back, her favorite perch. As she turned her head slowly from side to side, she took in the beautifully barren countryside of the remote island. The mists had retreated behind the clouds, and the sun shone down on the massive standing stones around them.

"Our time has come to an end." Her voice sounded a bit wistful.

She would miss this new place where she and Wolf had come to guide and be guided, to teach and to learn. She would miss Sarah, the friend who had helped them all to see the connections of their hearts.

Sarah, sensing Owl's sadness, held out her arm. Owl hopped from Wolf's deep warm fur onto Sarah's delicate arm. Sarah stroked her feathers gently, smiling. She bowed her head and whispered in Owl's ear. The big eyes gazed into the sweet face of the young woman in wonder, then Owl smiled and nodded.

"I understand."

Sarah held out her hands to the young men who had traveled with her through this long day, and they walked slowly toward her.

"How do we thank you?" asked Josh. "The things we have seen, everything we have learned, the stories we have shared…they will stay with us forever."

"There is no need of thanks. We were brought together, all of us, for a reason, just as all things happen for a reason. You just need to make a promise, a promise to not hold these things as your own, but to share them. This has been a wee bit of magic, a sampling of the lights and colors that exist here in this special place. You have been blessed, and now you must share the wonders you have seen."

As she hugged each of them, one by one, the gray mists began creeping back across the green hills toward the standing stones. She turned and walked toward the rolling darkness that approached.

Suddenly a thought came into Joe's head.

"Wait! I just remembered something." She hesitated, looking back over her shoulder. "Our great-great-granny's name was Sarah, just like yours."

She smiled a bright, wide smile, winking a twinkling eye at Owl.

"Yes, I know," she said, smiling as she stepped into the swirling mist.

Then she was gone.

EPILOGUE

Jeremy listened to his father's stories intently as they walked through the cool mountain air. Autumn had arrived, and there was already the promise of an early winter in the air. Scott had been anxious to get home to share the lessons he had learned with his young family.

Jeremy loved these times with Scott, when it was just the two of them. Mommy and his little sister had other things to do. That was when Daddy would take him into the mountain forest and talk to him about the animals and trees, how to read the stars and identify the tracks on the forest floor.

"It sounds so cool, Daddy. I wish I could go there!"

Scott knew, just as he had needed to take this journey, his son would need to walk those footsteps as well. Scott's mind wandered back, seeing the stones, the ruins, the mists, and the moors of that special land across the great water.

I hope he is the one, Scott thought quietly, holding the thought deep inside. *I hope he grows to understand how important it has all been.*

Scott turned to speak to his son, but Jeremy had stopped several yards behind him. There, at the foot of a towering pine tree, the little boy knelt slowly, peering into the piles of drying needles.

"Daddy, look!" Scott strode back to his young son and looked down.

There, lying in the lengthening shadows of the deep woods, he saw a tiny bird with a wing hanging limply at its side. The bird seemed only to see the little boy who reached down to gently retrieve him from where she lay.

Scott smiled in perfect understanding. As it should, the circle could begin again...

AUTHOR'S NOTES

This novel is a work of fiction and fantasy based on stories and legends handed down through time and family oral tradition. However, many of the characters in this book have been important in my life. They are not fictional creations, but rather wonderful and amazing people whose lives I have been honored to share. So, to three of my sons, a few of my many grandchildren, Jeremy and Sierra Kelty, Joey and Jack Sarcinella, and my children's friends, Jenny and Jason Kordak, I will be forever grateful. They have shown me that family crosses boundaries of time, space, and blood. Family is often born in the heart, not only in the blood.

I have always been thankful to my mother for sharing her father's Native American history and stories so I would be able to pass that honor and respect for our native heritage on to my own children. She also took pride in her maternal roots on the British Isles. My depiction of Sarah was based on her grandmother, my beloved, Great Granny. Sarah was a beautiful and feisty lady of English birth. And as Joe learned in this book, none of us would be the people we are were it not for the other half of our heritage. I must thank my Scottish father for reminding me we are of two great cultures. Much gratitude also goes to my friend, the very talented Celtic storyteller, Alice Natale, who helped me give voice to Sarah.

In 2016 a chance attendance at a lecture by Nick Card, the director of the Ness of Brodgar, piqued my interest in this very real and amazing site on the island of Orkney in the North Sea. After a brief discussion with him following his lecture, I knew I must be a part of the adventure he was leading.

The following summer, I sat in a little hut set on a slim neck of land thousands of miles from my home in the Arizona desert. It was here I met the delightful and incredibly knowledgeable Anne Mitchell, development project officer of the Ness of Brodgar. Within a day or two I was in love with the area, the history, the wonder, the imagination, and the science of the Ness. I knew the final piece of Wolf and Owl's journey must take them across the ocean. I also knew I wanted to be a part of the future of this endeavor, helping in some small way to ensure the continuation of the exploration. A portion of the proceeds of this book will be donated to this project. I requested Director Card write a short overview of the Ness of Brodgar for anyone interested in learning more about this archaeological treasure and the ancient history of the island of Orkney.

THE NESS OF BRODGAR

An Overview

*Nick Card, Director of the Ness of Brodgar
and LEADER Development Project*
University of Highlands and Islands Archaeology
Institute, Orkney College UHI

Off the northern tip of Scotland, lie the Orkney Islands where it is said if you scratch the surface, it bleeds archaeology. This is most evident in the middle of the main island where there are some of the most iconic prehistoric monuments in Europe: the two stone circles of the Ring of Brodgar and the Stones of Stenness; Maes Howe, the finest chambered tomb in northern Europe, plus other standing stones and prehistoric burial mounds. Together with Skara Brae, the best-preserved Neolithic village in Europe, these monuments were recognized as being of international importance in 1999 with their designation as a World Heritage Site, the Heart of Neolithic Orkney.

In the midst of this remarkable archaeological landscape, in March 2003 the Archaeology Institute of the University of the Highlands and Islands investigated the discovery of a strange, large, notched stone slab in a field on the Ness of Brodgar, a thin peninsula of land between the two stone circles.

Little could we imagine that this new discovery would lead to the uncovering of a site that would rival all these known monuments and revolutionize our understanding of many aspects of the Neolithic of Atlantic Europe.

Initial small-scale trial trenching around the site soon revealed that the massive mound that covers the tip of the Brodgar peninsula was not a natural geological formation as had been thought, but the product of over 1,200 years of human activity, spanning the whole of the Neolithic in Orkney from approximately 3,500 to 2,300 BC.

Although the excavations have now extended, our large trenches still cover less than 10% of the site. The mound was the product of the gradual accumulation of material from 60 generations of use: buildings being constructed, some falling out of use, several phases of new ones being built over the earlier ones, and rubbish and general waste building up. Hidden within this mound we have discovered a site like no other in northern Europe: a complex of many massive 5,000 year old buildings, partly enclosed by huge walls.

Unlike the contemporary domestic villages such as Skara Brae elsewhere in Orkney, the buildings at the Ness are truly monumental in scale and much more refined in their internal, regular and angular architecture. Externally these structures were also different as their roofs were covered with large stone slates, those at the Ness being the earliest yet discovered. The accomplished stonework is also enhanced by extensive decoration of incised, picked and pecked geometric designs (over 800 examples, more than all the rest of the UK combined!), the use of different colored sandstones, and the application of colored pigments to the stonework.

These structures were not intended to be lived in throughout the year but seem to have been special places perhaps with religious or ritual meaning. This was a place of pivotal importance to Neolithic Orkney. It was the heart of their world. It was a place of coming together for people from all over Orkney and likely from further afield. Why? For feasting, trading, gossiping, story-telling, performing rituals and above all else, for celebrating the important political and celestial events that defined the complex and vibrant society of the time.

The importance of the site is also reflected in its stone tools and pottery, for although many are replicated at other sites, the numbers of exceptional and exquisite examples such as polished stone axes and mace-heads, along with unusual items such as carved stone balls, are quite staggering. The pottery assemblage, dominated by 'Grooved Ware' (the name of its style), is also unusual not only in the scale of the collection (over 90,000 pieces (sherds)) but also the wide range of decorative motifs it exhibits, including the use of color.

Finds from the Ness also reflect the non-insular nature of the site and its wider connections: pitchstone (a volcanic glass like obsidian) from Arran off the SW coast of Scotland; axes from the Lake District in northern England; mace heads from the Western Isles of Scotland: art only paralleled in Ireland; amber from the east coast of Scotland, and a style of pot only found elsewhere around Stonehenge.

Even the associated main trash heap that lies just outside the southern wall is monumental at over 70 metres in diameter and surviving to over 5 metres in height (no doubt much reduced in scale from when it was made). This consists of mainly peat ash cleared from innumerable cooking fires lit at the Ness, and the rubbish generated from the feasts made when large gatherings occurred. The creation of this mound seems to be making its own statement about the Ness, for all to see. It reflects the conspicuous consumption that was, no doubt, a large part of the activity at the Ness.

Everything about the Ness clearly states that this was an exceptional and special place. The excavation and all the subsequent post-excavation analysis has only been possible with a lot of hard work, support and input from a whole host of individuals and bodies—too many to name individually here. The Ness team is made up of professionals, students and volunteers, many of whom give up their own time to assist, and the efforts of that team are very gratefully acknowledged. Much gratitude too, to John and Carol Hoey for original access to the south of the Ness, and to Arnie and Ola Tait for continued access to their land. Without their and your support we could not carry on.

The work at the Ness of Brodgar is mainly supported by public donation. By purchasing this book, you are helping this ground-breaking research to continue—Thank you. We do hope that you will visit and further support us—who knows what riches the Ness will reveal which will further rewrite prehistory? Follow us through our website nessofbrodgar.com where you will also find details of our US charity the American Friends of the Ness of Brodgar (501)©(3) charitable organization, ID 31954, IRS No 46/4020309